D1394587

SIC TRANSIT WAGON

ACKNOWLEDGEMENTS

These stories first appeared in the following publications:
"It's Cherry Pink and Apple Blossom White", *Wasafiri* Vol. 26, No 1. Issue no. 65 Spring 2011; "Ghost Story", *Small Axe*, No. 38, Vol. 16/2, 2012, Duke University Press; "It's not where you go it's how you get there", in *Moving Right Along*, Lexicon, Trinidad, 2010; "Gold Bracelets", *The Caribbean Writer*, Volume 24, 2010; and "The Talisman", *The Caribbean Writer*, Volume 26, 2012.

BARBARA JENKINS

SIC TRANSIT WAGON

AND OTHER STORIES

PEEPAL TREE

First published in Great Britain in 2013
Peepal Tree Press Ltd
17 King's Avenue
Leeds LS6 1QS
England

ISBN13: 9781845232146

Supported using public funding by
ARTS COUNCIL
ENGLAND

For my mother, Yvonne Lafond,
and my husband, Paul Jenkins

Better late than never

CONTENTS

1.

Curtains   11
It's Cherry Pink and Apple Blossom White   17
Maybe Tomorrow Will Be Better   26
The Day the Earth Stood Still   39
I Never Heard Pappy Play the Hawaiian Guitar   49
Gold Bracelets   57

2.

Monty and Marilyn   67
The Talisman   75
It's Not Where You Go, It's How You Get There   91
Across the Gulf   101
Ghost Story   112

3.

Erasures   125
To-may-to / To-mah-to   133
Making Pastelles in Dickensland   143
A Perfect Stranger   155
Sic Transit Wagon   159

1

CURTAINS

That day the breeze was blowing more strongly than usual, or perhaps it was blowing at its usual strength, but I had no reason to notice it before. The long, white curtains that hung from the top of the doorframes had shaken themselves loose of the ribbons that restrained them and were swelling with breeze in and out, lifting over and flapping with soft slaps against the chairs and tables in the gallery, filling the spaces of the wide-open doorways – doorways so wide, so high, that Uncle would have me, just three years old, sitting astride his shoulders, clinging hard to the reins of his hair, while he galloped me, wildly shrieking with fear and excitement, from bedroom to gallery to another bedroom to gallery to living room to kitchen. In and out the dusty bluebells, he would sing, dancing me from one room to the next, through the encircling gallery of my grandmother's home that was my home too, with my mother and her brothers.

The curtain, full of wind, billowed over my bed that day, brushing a feathery tickle across my face, waking me earlier than usual. I opened my eyes and looked around for my mother but she was not in our bedroom. I did not call for her because, when I listened to the world I had just woken up to, I could hear her voice and my grandmother's voice coming from the gallery, just outside our bedroom. There was something slow and serious about the voices, one after the other, which made my own voice stay quiet while pulling me towards theirs. I slid down off the big bed and stood behind one of the curtains. That hard, strong breeze bellied the curtain. It wrapped itself round me, hiding me in its long folds as I stood in the doorway, watching and listening. The thin, pale day drew only faint broken lines of light through the waving branches and leaves of the big chenette tree outside, but I could see the back of my grandmother's dress with its printed yellow flowers on leafy green vines peeping through the woven cane of her rocking chair, her long grey plait swinging from side to side over the back of the chair as she rocked back and forth, back and forth. The rockers went squeak, bump, squeak, bump, against the hard mahogany floor with a rhythm so regular that, even if I closed my eyes, I could tell when the next squeak, the next bump, was coming. My mother was standing in front of the rocking chair, facing my grandmother and facing me too, but she couldn't see me where I was hiding. She was wearing her white housedress with pink and blue flowers sprinkled all over it and big pockets and a big round collar edged with white lace.

Through the blurriness of the curtain, I could see her head bent down and I could see her arms only down to her elbows. I imagined her holding her hands together behind her back, her fingers twisting round and round the ring she wore on her right hand, the ring with the blue stone she said was her birthstone. She always did that ring twisting when her hands were behind her back. I wanted to go out to the gallery, to stand near my mother, but there was something strange about the way they held their bodies, apart and stiff, the way they spoke to each other, as if they were not the same mother, the same grandmother that I had left when I fell asleep the night before, and it held me back, made me silent and secretive. My grandmother was speaking. She spoke for a long time. Her voice was not loud but it came out solid and hard like a plank of wood – a plank of wood with knotholes and rough patches. I understood only some of what she said… not again… shame… make your own bed and lie in it.

I wondered why she was talking so seriously about making a bed. I knew my mother hadn't made our bed yet – I had been asleep there until a little while before. Why should that make my grandmother so vexed as to quarrel with my mother? My mother spoke softly and only for a little time, not interrupting but taking her turn. I could hear none of her words. Her voice did not have its usual up and down curves. It was just flat and soft and down. She was not looking at my grandmother – she was looking down at her feet and that made her words fall to the floor. Was not making your bed and lying on it such a naughty thing to do? I felt a strong urge to go out to the gallery and stand with my mother and hold on to the tail of her housedress to show that I too was sorry about the not making of the bed, but, at the same time, I sensed that the talking was somehow about important big people business and I should not interrupt. I was afraid that if I went out there to them they would be angry with me and I would be scolded and sent off to Cooksy in the kitchen.

When I got tired of standing I sat on the floor, near to one of the giant hooks in the wall that held open the big glass-paned doors. I ran my hand along the cold, hard hook. I pushed my fingers alongside the head of the hook, into the round metal circle screwed into the door. I wanted to pull out the head of the hook and free the door. My grandmother, uncles and mother had all warned me, from the time I could crawl about, that I was not to unhook the doors or they would slam shut in the breeze, breaking the glass, sending splinters flying everywhere, especially into my eyes and I would go blind. I used to walk about the gallery with my eyes shut, stumbling into furniture, practising how I would get around if one day I disobeyed, the glass shattered and I went blind. I wanted to unhook the door, so that the door would slam shut, and then they would stop the talking, because I didn't like how I felt when I heard my mother's voice, so soft and having no tune in it. But I did not lift the hook out of the metal circle, even though I wanted to. Instead I stood up and paid attention to the talking again which had got so soft I couldn't make out any words at all.

My mother looked up at my grandmother and said something that must have been a question because her voice rose up at the end. The rocking chair stopped. The soles of my grandmother's slippers made a slap on the floor as she leaned forward and put her feet down. She shook her head from side to side. My mother looked down at her own feet again. She slowly turned away and walked towards our bedroom, but she didn't see me because I was still wrapped in the curtain and standing very still and quiet. I saw her look at the bed, at where I usually slept. Maybe she was looking for me. Then she went and sat at the foot of the bed. She sat with her chin resting on her hand, her elbow propped on her knee. She looked down at her lap, glanced back at the bed, then turned around again. Maybe she thought I was at breakfast in the kitchen with Cooksy. Her back to me, she looked straight ahead, right into the mirror of the dressing table that she was facing. She could not have been really looking into the mirror or she would've seen me, the lumpy ghost in the curtain I saw reflected in the mirror's wide silver face.

She stared and stared ahead and then she dropped her face into her hands. I could see her shoulders shaking and I could hear her going… huhhh… huhhhhn… huhhh… huhnnn, as if she was squeezing her voice inside, trying to hold it back, but some of it pushed its way out anyway. I felt an ache in my chest. I didn't understand what was going on. I wanted to hug her and make it all right, but I didn't know how to let her know that I was hiding in the curtain for she would realise I had been looking on and listening all along, and I thought she wouldn't like that, so I just stayed quiet where I was.

After a long while, she leaned forward, pulled open a drawer, took out a handkerchief and blew her nose in it. She looked again into the drawer and started taking things out of it and throwing them over her shoulders on to the bed. In a great hurry, she pulled open all the drawers, one by one, and did the same thing, flinging everything on our bed behind her, not seeming to care where they landed. Sheer stockings and the grey elastic rings that held them up, her panties and brassieres and girdle, her yellow nightie and the white one, her flesh-coloured silky petticoats and half-slips flew out, undoing their soft, careful folds and piling up in an untidy heap. My clothes came out too – white vests and panties and socks, flowery seersucker pyjamas. When she was done with the drawers, she pushed them shut and sat a while doing nothing. Then, she stood and walked slowly to the wardrobe and, from it she lifted out clothes on hangers, looking at each item – the blue silk dress with smocking at the front that I loved to look at, trying to work out how the stitching was done; the green taffeta one that made wavy patterns of light and shade running up and down it when she walked in it, that made me think of dragonflies tipping their heads to ripple the mossy pond at the Botanic Gardens; her slippery blouse with long see-through sleeves, and the floppy polka-dot one with a floppy bow at the front; a grey pleated skirt and a stiff narrow black one with slits on the sides. Then she lifted out my dresses – the plaid dress with the wide red sash for going for walks, and the yellow organdie one for church. All of these she touched – a collar of one, a lacy edge of another, a sash, a bow, then placed them with slow care on the bed.

She looked at the bed, her eyes moving over the heaps and the piles of things there, and turning away abruptly, she walked through the door that connected our room to Uncle's bedroom. I could hear her talking with Uncle and a little while after she came back with a big brown grip that she put on the bed. When she lifted some little gold catches, the grip popped open in two halves. One by one she folded all the clothes that were on the bed, put them into the grip, went out the room again and came back with a paper bag that had handles; she put that on the bed too. From her dressing-table top, she took her hairbrush and comb, the round box with pink face powder and the square one with white body powder and its fluffy puff that made you sneeze, and put them in the paper bag. The little tortoiseshell box with her jewellery went into her white handbag, which she then snapped shut. I hadn't noticed when she put the handbag on the bed. She opened the handbag again and took out a small-change purse. She twisted open the top and looked inside, took a roll of paper money from the brassiere she was wearing and put it in the change purse, clicked it shut and put it in the handbag, closing that too. Then she opened it again and took out a tube of lipstick. She twisted the tube and ran the red tip of lipstick over her mouth without looking in the mirror as she usually did. She put back the lipstick and shut the handbag once more.

Digging into the brown paper bag, she pulled out the comb and dragged it through her hair. It met a tangle and she tugged at it until the tangle came out along with a few long strands which she pulled off the comb, rolled into a ball and dropped on the dressing table. She opened the handbag again, took out the tortoiseshell box, opened it and picked out a pair of gold earrings, the ones that hang down with an oval coin with a flat statue of a lady in a long dress and veil on it. I looked to see if she would take out and wear the gold bracelets that she always kept in that box, but she did not.

She put back the tortoiseshell box and closed the handbag, opened the wardrobe and pulled out a pair of white shoes – the ones with peep holes at the front where you could see her big toes. Next, she opened the grip and took out a pair of stockings and the elastic circles and closed the grip. She put on the stockings and the elastics, stood up, bent her head round to look at the back of her legs and put on the shoes. She opened the grip and put the slippers she had been wearing into the grip and closed it again. When she looked down at her housedress, she stopped for a bit, then she began to pull it off in a hurry, lifting it over her head. She opened the grip and took out the stiff narrow skirt and pulled it on. The zip wouldn't go right up and she left it like that, halfway done, while she scrambled around in the grip and took out the girdle, stepped into in, wiggling and wiggling until she pulled it right up under the skirt. Then she bent her head, looked at the waist of the skirt and finished pulling up the zip. I could see the floppy polka-dot blouse with the floppy bow right on top the things in the grip. She just threw that blouse on. The floppy bow was not even; one tail hung lower than the other, but she didn't seem to notice. She did not look at herself in the mirror, not even once.

My mother picked up the handbag and walked out the door, right past where I was hidden in the curtain, across the gallery. I could hear the heels of her shoes going toc, toc, toc down the long flight of concrete steps, the sound getting fainter and fainter until there was no more sound. I stayed shrouded in the caul of that curtain for a long, long time, looking through it at the brown grip and the paper bag and the thrown-off housedress curled up on the bed. I stayed there waiting, listening for the toc, toc, toc to come back.

IT'S CHERRY PINK AND APPLE BLOSSOM WHITE

When I was eleven, my family split up. I didn't know then and I don't know now what caused this to happen. All I know is that one day my mother said that we were going to stay with some other people. It was right after I had taken the Exhibition exam for a high school place; the school holiday was about to begin and I remember my confusion as we children always spent the six weeks of holidays with our grandmother, at my mother's childhood home in Belmont Valley.

Maybe our father had decided he wouldn't continue to pay rent for our three rooms in the house in Boissiere Village. He didn't live with us, he visited in erratic pouncings. When his car slid silently to a halt at the house, the message, *Yuh fadda reach*, ran through the neighbourhood and, wherever we were, we scampered home. He sat on the bed, pointing to his left cheek for us to kiss and I wished for sudden death rather than enter his aura of smoke, staleness and rum. My mother made him coffee. One of us carried it to him. He drank it and left. Without his support, perhaps my mother saw the scattering of her brood as her only option when she no longer had a home in which we could all live together.

When she told me we would be going somewhere else, I got a cold, hard clenching feeling in my belly, but I didn't have the words to tell her that. As she was leaving, she stood facing me, held my shoulders and said, "Be a good girl," as she did whenever she left me anywhere, but that time my mother didn't look into my eyes; she looked down at the floor. I saw her cheeks were smeared and wet; I was puzzled. I touched her face; the powder she rarely wore came off on my palm. She was dressed as if for a special occasion, a christening or a funeral, and, as she turned away, I caught hold of the skirt of her smoke-grey shantung dress with the tiny pearl buttons like a row of boiled fishes' eyes. My hand left a dull orange smear of Max Factor Suntan. I saw the stain I had made and I felt glad.

None of us was left with family. I was to go to a neighbour; one sister was sent to San Fernando to stay with friends of my mother's – people we children didn't know; where the other went I don't remember, but I do know that our mother took only my one-year-old brother with her, and we didn't know where. I think that she must have been planning this for a while; the far-flung arrangements would have been difficult to negotiate quickly without telephone, and the timing was too convenient to be coincidence.

My new home was a shop. Over the street door was a sign, white lettering on black, "Marie Tai Shue, licensed to sell spirituous liquors". I knew the shop well, since, as the eldest, I was the one sent to make message. We children on the making message mission scrambled up with dusty bare feet to sit on the huge hundredweight crocus bags of dry goods stacked against the interior walls of the shop until Auntie Marie called out, "What you come for?" Nobody but the bees cared that we were sitting on foodstuffs – rice, sugar, dried beans, and the bees only bothered if you sat on a sugar bag without noticing their plump golden-brown stripes camouflaged against the brown string of the sacks, heads burrowed into the tight weave.

Early morning, my mother sent me for four hops bread and two ounces of cheese or salami; mid-morning, half-pound rice, quarter-pound dried beans, quarter-pound pig tail, salt beef or salt fish; more hops bread and two ounces of fresh butter mid-afternoon. I had no money for my shopping; we took goods "on trust" all week. The items were handed over, the amount owed was noted in Chinese script on a small square of brown paper selected from a creased and curling pack threaded through a long hooked wire suspended from a nail driven into the back wall. I would peer over the counter to watch Auntie go to the dark recesses of the shop, hear the thunk of the chopper as it cleaved through the salted meat into the chopping block, then remember

18

to call, "Mammie say cut from the middle," or "Mammie say not too much bone." On Saturdays, my mother went herself for the week's supplies: Nestlé's condensed milk, Fry's cocoa powder, bars of yellow Sunlight soap for washing clothes and a single-cup sachet of Nestle instant coffee, just in case. She'd bring a rum bottle for cooking oil and a can for pitch-oil for the stove. What she was able to take away depended on Auntie's goodwill and on how much of that week's accumulated "on trust" total she could wipe off.

In my new life I was on the other side of the shop counter with a new family. The six children ranged in age from fifteen to nine. I moved in with a cardboard box and a folding canvas camp-bed which the boys set up in the girls' room, between Suelin's bed and Meilin's and Kanlin's double-decker. One of the boys hammered two new nails behind the bedroom door where my clothes would hang alongside the girls': a Sunday dress, two outgrown school overalls as day clothes and another for the night. That first night, I closed my eyes and saw pictures running behind my eyelids. I saw my cousins at my grandmother's climbing trees, picking and eating chenette, mango, pommerac, playing in the rain and the river. Without me. I saw Miriam, chief rival as my grandmother's favourite, brushing Granny's long silver hair until she fell asleep at siesta-time. Perhaps, with me not there, Uncle Francois was choosing Jeannie to help him pack the panniers of gladioli and dahlias to take to the flower shop. I felt red heat rise and fill my head at my mother for cheating me of what was mine by right. Then I remembered her face when she was leaving me. I wondered why she wouldn't look at me. Did she feel bad about leaving me where I didn't want to be? I felt a tugging tightness in my throat about being glad for spoiling her best dress. I had looked at her downcast face and promised I would be a good girl and not give Auntie Marie any trouble.

Life in my new home seemed one of plenty – the whole grocery to choose from, a shower with a door and latch, toothpaste not salt, their own latrine. I felt lucky. All these luxuries were mine too. On dry days, Meilin and I scrubbed clothes in a tub and spread soapy garments on a bed of rocks in the backyard to bleach in the sunshine. Next day, two of the boys rinsed and wrung out the clothes, draping them over hibiscus and sweet lime bushes to dry. Between us we swept and mopped the floors of the two bedrooms and the common living and dining space at the back of the shop where Auntie slept at night in a hammock of bleached flourbags. After closing the shop at night, Auntie cooked dinner, my first experience of strange food: grainy rice or noodles infused with the salt and fat of chunks of Chinese sausage, patchoi, cabbage, carrots fragrant with thin slices of ginger steamed in a bamboo basket above the simmering pot, meat slivers flashed in a wok. Auntie spoke Cantonese to her children; they answered in English. I listened to tone, looked from face to face, followed the thread and joined in.

The bigger children helped in the shop; I wasn't expected to, but I often sat on a bench, watching and listening and learning. I could fold brown paper so that the edges were straight and, inserting a long, sharp knife, cut to size for half-pound, quarter-pound, two-ounce dry goods and farthing salt, but two tricks of the trade defeated me. The first was twisting a sheet of paper up at two sides around dry goods to make a firm, leak-proof package and flipping the whole over to close the top in a fold. The second was unpicking the ends of the stitching across the top of a crocus bag so that, when you held the two loose ends of string and pulled, the top of the bag fell open to expose sugar or rice, like Moses unzipping the Red Sea to reveal the dry land below, leaving you with a long zigzag piece of twine, perfect for flying kites.

I had long idle spells when I would read – anything, everything. On the narrow shelves along the shop's back wall were goods we seldom had at home. I would pick up these luxuries, hold them, read the labels: Carnation evaporated milk, Libby's corned beef, blue and gold tins of fresh butter, Andrex toilet paper, Moddess sanitary napkins. My hands caressed things from England, Australia, New Zealand, USA and I felt a current connecting me with those places. The boys had comic books that they hid under their beds. I would borrow a comic and steal away to read it quickly and borrow another. Comics pulled me immediately into their unambiguous graphic world where I had the power to do anything. I could save the world from alien invasion, rescue beleaguered innocents from danger, fight forces bent on destroying civilisation. With just Kryptonite, a Batmobile, a two-way wrist radio, Hi-Ho Silver, I leapt over skyscrapers with a single bound, stopped speeding trains with bare hands, deflected bullets to ricochet onto the bad guys, big things, real things. When I stopped reading, I looked at my world, hoping to find some disaster I could avert, but I saw no Martians, missiles or maverick trains, so I opened another comic, and another. I lived in so many other worlds that, for much of the time, I moved through my real world as if it was just something else I was reading and had got lost in. Each new thing I read added to my world, making my own life something I had to let happen, like a story whose pages I was turning, not something I could shape myself.

For the people I lived with, reading brought them the world they had physically left but had carried with them in everything they thought and did. The Chinese community had an informal circulating library of magazine-type papers from China, "Free" China. Auntie and Suelin would read the Chinese script from the back page bottom right corner and work their way up the columns to the front page. From the synopsis in English, I learnt about Sun-Yat-Sen, saw pictures of Chiang-Kai-Shek with the glamorous cheongsam-clad Madam Chiang-Kai-Shek, and read about Mao-Tse-Tung. The first two were revered, the last hated – he and the Communists had driven them out of China, stealing all they had and then seizing their family. I wondered whether the Communists had captured my mother, forcing her to give us away and if this was so, how did she know that the people she left me with could be trusted not to give me to the Communists in exchange for their own captured family? I didn't think they would do this because they were taking care of me, just as if I was one of the children of their family. But then, maybe they were fattening me up like the witch in Hansel and Gretel, because sometimes they had big gatherings and feasts.

When fellow shopkeepers, laundry owners and restaurant proprietors came to visit on Sunday, the white-shirted men and their jade-bedecked wives would sit round a table quickly assembled from an old door and packing cases, covered with a white sheet. Competing chatter in passionate, high-pitched Cantonese – sounds like frantic trapped birds crashing into glass panes –

would rise to a clamour, and just when I thought a fight would start, there would be explosions of laughter, the brandishing of magazines, and the pointing at one another with raised chopsticks, still pinching slick black mushrooms and floppy white wantons. There was a constant flow of china bowls and platters bearing translucent rice noodles and bright green chopped chives floating in clear broth, shrimp and pork fried rice, meat, soybean curd, bamboo shoots, water chestnuts, glistening roasted duck, rice wine poured from a ceramic bottle into matching thimble cups, sweet and sour prunes hidden in layers of paper, preserved ginger. I had never been to a restaurant, had never imagined such plenty of food and noise. I had never before seen this close-knittedness, this exclusiveness of clan bonding. I stayed on the edge, watching. I felt I was both in and at a movie.

On a normal weekday I found other entertainment, watching bar customers. Men came in from mid-morning, ordered shots of rum and single cigarettes, sat on long benches at the wooden table to drink, smoke, play cards for small stakes, talk, argue. On payday they would buy nips and flasks, pour on the dusty concrete floor an offering to those gone before, and lime as long as they could until their women sent children to rescue the residue of the family funds before it was all smoked, drunk and gambled away. We in-house children served the orders, cleared up glasses and ran our own riotous card games in a corner with burnt matches as our stakes.

But best of all was the radio in the bar, a novelty for me. It was kept permanently tuned to WVDI, beamed from the American base at Chaguaramas. The call signal, "This is station WVDI, the armed forces radio station in Trinidad", was said in that cool, confident, leisurely, Yankee drawl that conjured up other lives entitled to Wrigley's Spearmint chewing gum, soda fountains, high school sweaters emblazoned with huge single letters, driving on the right side of the road in a convertible, hair blowing in the wind. That year, Perez Prado and his Cuban Orchestra dominated the airwaves with his number one hit, "It's Cherry Pink and Apple Blossom White". Twenty times a day or more, a trumpet wailed the opening bars, that long sustained waaaaaaah, a puppet string of sound, pulling me to my feet, making me forget who, what, where, lifting me into that upswelling blare. I was Scarlett O'Hara, smooth thick black hair curling round shoulders, long slender fingers curved into back of the neck of someone like Rhett Butler, his smouldering eyes scorching mine; my True Romance magazine figure was draped in a V-necked cowl with a flared skirt which swirled and lifted as we two, entranced, mamboed across the dance floor lost to the admiration and applause of all.

When the song was over, Meilin and I, panting with exertion, would collapse on a bench and she would tell me about her school. She had been in high school since last year, when a neighbour brought the newspaper to Auntie Marie to show her that Meilin's name was there, that she had passed the Exhibition exam. Auntie Marie couldn't read English, and she called Meilin to read her own name, to make sure. I wondered if my name would be on the list when the results came out. I wondered how I would know, how my mother would know, as we didn't buy papers. As we talked about Meilin's school, I wasn't sure I liked the sound of it – Bishop's. Their uniform had a funny hat with pointy corners that made them look like the soldiers in history books about Napoleon. St Joseph's Convent girls wore floating white veils and looked like they were little nuns already on their way to heaven. Also, Bishop's girls had gym twice a week and afterwards showered together. This bothered me.

"Does that mean people could see your punky and totots?"

"After a while, people don't bother to look. You get accustomed."

I'd have to do very well in the exam to win a free place at either school – if I only passed, my mother couldn't pay fees like Meilin's. We made a pact. If I won first place, I told her, I would choose her school. We hooked the little fingers of our right hands to seal this pledge. At times like those, Meilin shared with me her burgeoning knowledge of life. She told me about her monthly bleeding and I said it wouldn't happen to me. She told me what men and women did in secret and I didn't believe her. She told me that babies came out through their mothers' punkies and I knew then that she was just making it all up. We danced through that long holiday, we and Perez Prado singing, "It's cherry pink and apple blossom white, when your true lover comes your way". It was about flowers we had never seen, emotions we were too young to understand.

I had seen or heard nothing about my family for a long time, when, one day at the end of August, my Uncle Francois raced up on his bicycle with a bunch of purple and white dahlias in the basket. He gave the flowers to Auntie Marie and the two of them whispered together, glancing towards me while they shush-shushed. I wondered what I had done wrong. He called out, "Get ready. Your mother coming for you." Auntie gave me one of her precious brown paper carrier bags. I put my clothes in it and waited. When I first saw my mother, I thought it was my aunt, her twin sister. Her long hair was gone; she looked older, more nervous than I remembered. She looked at me, said, "You got bigger," squeezed me tight, patted my head, sat me in the back seat of the waiting car. We were taken to La Seiva, where my grand-mother had moved without my knowing. Two men were waiting there for me: a photographer and a reporter. The results of the Exhibition exam were released to the newspaper and my mother had been tracked down through my Uncle Francois, whose flower-growing business everybody knew. I was to be photo-graphed and interviewed for the next day's *Guardian* because I had come first in the College Exhibition exam. Afterwards, Uncle Francois bought a jug of coconut ice cream from a passing vendor's bike-cart, a special treat for me.

The news must have reached our father somehow, because that night he arrived in La Seiva. He and my mother spoke in the gallery for a long time. I don't know for sure why they decided to get back together. Maybe the people to whom we children had been sent had agreed to keep us only for the school holidays. I also think that when the news of my success became public, our father would have felt ashamed among his friends and co-workers, shown up as a man who didn't take care of his children. Our father said he had found somewhere for us to live. He took my mother and me to see the place.

It was in Belmont, two bare rooms at the back of a house. The partition walls of wood with open slats at the top allowed air, sound and smell to circulate freely between the rooms, already home to two other watching, listening families. Standing in the backyard, I took in the dank open-air shower, its door hanging on a single hinge. In the kitchen-shed, coal-pot charcoal sparked red eyes through black smoke; from the sink, grey water splashed into a mossy open drain where, in a crack, a cluster of ambitious tomato seedlings had rooted. My nose trailed the pit latrine to its location, under the silhouetted tracery of branches and leaves of a guava tree at the back of the house. I could touch the neighbour's crumbling house over the sagging galvanised fence; I could hear the wail of a child, a hot, heavy slap – "Here is something to cry for!" – the heightened wailing. My mother looked straight ahead, silent, hewn. I do not think she saw, heard or smelled anything. I saw her shoulders straighten; I felt mine straighten too.

Next day, we separated children were re-gathered. As silent as strangers, we moved into our new life in the open tray of a Ford truck alongside my mother's other possessions: a two-burner pitch-oil stove, an iron cooking pot, two cardboard boxes of clothes, one of crockery, and her girlhood treasures – a foot-pedal Singer sewing machine and a grand matching bedroom set of solid mahogany: bed, dressing table, stool and wardrobe. All, like us, had been looked after somewhere. My picture was in the papers. I was soon to go to big school. I was a big girl now.

MAYBE TOMORROW WILL BE BETTER

The girl dashes out of the room as soon as Miss dismisses class. She is so fizzing with excitement at the news Miss just gave that, as she skips along the pavement on her way home, she breaks into a spontaneous hopscotch, *step on a crack, break your mother's back.* Miss said, *hop-one-two,* Miss told the class, *three-four-five,* that next week Friday, *six-seven,* they would be having, *jump-and-spin-aroun*d, a party, *hop-back-again,* a Christmas party. *Seven-six, five-four-th*... mid-hop she stops, puzzled. A Christmas party? Is there such a thing as a Christmas party?

She thinks she knows all about Christmas. It's her favourite time of the year. Christmas is fixing up the house nicely with fresh paint, new curtains and cushion covers, neighbours, friends and family in new clothes visiting to eat Mammy's black cake, drink sorrel and ginger beer, laugh, tell jokes, play games and enjoy themselves, children singing carols around the crèche and Father Christmas coming. But that's not having a party. That's just what happens at Christmas. She knows about having *birthday* parties, like her own.

Last Sunday was her birthday. Mammy invited the neighbours for ice cream and cake. The big girls turned the handle of the ice cream churn while the little ones ran around, sticking out their tongues to catch the cold chips, sparkly like diamonds, that sprayed from the shilling-block of ice as Mammy stabbed at it with the forbidden ice pick, chiselling out bigger, glittering chunks, packing them between the metal churn and the wooden bucket, then pouring salt, a fine, white stream, onto the ice. Miss Gibbs, who had a modern gas stove with built-in-oven, baked a sponge cake and put ten tiny yellow-and-white candles on it. The cake was iced in white and edged with a frill of green leaves and pink icing-sugar roses, roses that were too precious to eat, and were kept in the wire-meshed food safe. (Some months afterwards, Mammy followed a thick trail of red ants along the floor, up one leg of the safe, through the mesh to their feast: pink, melted, sticky puddles, no longer looking like roses. But that was long after.) At the birthday party, the girl stroked with a hesitant fingertip, the clean, sharp edge of a curled rose petal, lost in wonder that such perfection could come from the hands of an ordinary person, someone whom she knew. At the party, people ate cake and ice cream, sang *Happy Birthday To You*; children played musical chairs, chased one another in hoop until it was too dark to see and Mammy called them in from the yard for their mothers to take them home. Would a Christmas party be like that? As she continues along the pavement, the regular clack-clack-clack of her ruler, dragged along the high cast-iron railings that surround the big houses on the street, keeps time with her thoughts.

She supposes that a Christmas party would really be a birthday party for Jesus. How many candles would the cake have? Jesus died a long time ago. It seems strange to have a birthday party for someone who is dead. Her grandpa is dead. He died before she was even born – she doesn't know what day his birthday is. How is it that she knows, that people everywhere know, when Jesus' birthday is, who died hundreds and hundreds of years ago and she doesn't know her grandpa's birthday and he died only a short while ago? She will ask Miss tomorrow. Then she remembers that Miss had said something else. Something so important that she had said it twice to make sure everyone heard and understood. Miss said that everybody, everybody, had to buy a present and wrap it in pretty paper. All the presents would be put together in a big bag. Miss said each girl would then pull out one present, not the one she brought, from the bag, like from a bran tub in the bazaar. The whole thing is most strange. A Christmas present that doesn't come from Father Christmas? And a present before Christmas Eve night?

At her birthday party, nobody brought a present. People only brought themselves. She smiles – presence is presents. Words are magic, she thinks; they can exchange meaning when you're not looking. What she would have to exchange at the party is not words but a present. How would she do that? Maybe she could use magic? The most magical word of all, as everyone knows, is "Abracadabra". In books there are magicians who can wave a wand and things appear and disappear just by saying that word aloud. Could that word bring a present to exchange in a flash? She closes her eyes and says it aloud, "Abracadabra!" When she opens her eyes and there is no prettily wrapped package on the pavement in front of her, she is really not surprised because she doesn't have the magic wand.

A sweet-lime hedge has pushed through the railings further on, and, as she runs her ruler along, it bruises the tiny white flower clusters, sending up a sudden piercing sharp-sweet citrus scent which causes her to pause and bury her face in the crushed blossoms, inhaling their fragrance. But she starts back when, from the other side of the fence, two dogs snarl, forcing their muzzles through the hedge, baring their teeth, trying to snatch her ruler. "Stop that stupidness, child," comes a loud, stern voice; then, spoken more softly, more conciliatorily, "Madam, is only those children from the school down the road. They don't have no brought-upsy." Through a gap in the hedge she sees the speaker, a woman, whose features are lost in the shade of a big tree. She seems to be wrapped in a big, startlingly white apron. The little white cap perched on her head reminds the girl of the nurses in the Colonial Hospital where she had spent two weeks because of the long red ridges that rose like tram tracks wherever her nails scratched her skin. The doctor said it was a deficiency, but everybody else said it was "mad blood". The doctor gave her an iron injection in her bottom every other day. She thinks the iron must have settled under the needle pricks because she has still got eight hard black and blue bruises, big like pennies. But not the kind of pennies she would need to buy a present to take to the class party. She smiles at her own silly thought.

The woman in the cap and apron is pushing a little girl on a swing. The little girl looks like one of the cherub angels in St Francis Church. She is pink. Her soft, soft yellow hair lifts like wings behind her when the swing goes forward. Her pink hands hold on to the swing chain and the frilled hem of her white see-through dress hangs down from the seat. Red ribbon threads its way like red dashes through white eyelet lace around the puffed-sleeve cuffs and the rounded collar. A wide red ribbon is tied in a big red bow at the back of her waist and its ends float up behind her. On her stuck-out feet are red shoes with a cross-strap and white socks folded over at her ankles. She looks like something from a fairytale storybook. Storybook… she muses… a storybook is a good present. She has one at home. Father Christmas brought it last Christmas. The little girl's high, clear voice cuts through, "Push harder, Mabel. Push harder!" She continues on to the end of the school street where it meets the wide, busy road that runs around the Savannah.

Look right, look left, look right again, she chants, crossing the road to the pitch walk. Today there are three men sitting on a bench under the cannon ball tree. They call out to her as she passes by, "Chick, chick, how is the chickie today?" She pretends not to hear. Mammy has warned her not to talk to strange men. Are these strange men? She doesn't know them, but she sees them every day. Mammy has also said that she mustn't be rude to big people. Is walking fast and not answering being rude? Pappy may think so. He has told her that those men are special taxi drivers who take guests from the big hotel wherever they want to go and, as Pappy drives a taxi too, he may be friends with them. Pappy knows about hotels. He told her that when people who stay at the hotel go to the dining room, they have a list of food to choose from. She was amazed.

"I wouldn't choose. I would say, just bring everything."

"And how you paying for that, Missy?"

"You mean you have to pay? Even if you living there?"

"In life, you have to pay for everything."

She supposes, as she rattles her ruler along the savannah railings, when you small, is big people who have to pay for everything. Just last week, the man from Sports and Games came in the yard asking for Mammy and when she said that Mammy not there, the man asked whether that was her mother's bicycle and when she said yes, he said, "Yuh Mammy behind on the payments, so I taking back the bike." When Mammy came home, she just flopped down on the steps, like the tyre on the front wheel of the bicycle that had been left home that day only because it had a puncture. She said, "The Lord doesn't give you more than you can bear."

Would asking Mammy for money to buy an exchange present be giving her more than she could bear? If Mammy doesn't have the money, then she, not the Lord, would be giving her more that she could bear. The Lord knows about everything that is going to happen to you before you know it yourself. Maybe he would step in before the load gets too heavy? Could she depend on the Lord to be paying attention at that very moment and warn her? But he was so busy with everyone to look after and she was so small that she may not matter enough to get his attention. All this guessing is making her head feel confused.

She crosses from the savannah to the Queen's Park Café, *look right, look left, look right again.* She hurries past to avoid seeing the tempting toolum, Kaiser balls and tamarind balls in the glass case – she has already spent her penny on a guava syrup press. *Ah want ah penny to buy tambran ball, Kaiser ball. Gimmee a penny to buy tambran ball, Kaiser ball*, she sings to herself as she skips round the corner. She stops at the bridge over the Dry River, climbs onto the lower rail and leans over, looking down at the trickle of water in the inner channel of the paved riverbed. Some boys are playing bat and ball down there, using a stone and a coconut branch. Mammy warned her to keep away from stone throwing. *Stone don't have eyes.*

Miss Carmichael's granddaughter, Esmé, has one real eye and one glass eye. Miss Carmichael has not spoken to her son-in-law for eight years because a nail he was hammering into a piece of wood glanced off from under the hammer and caught Esmé's right eye when she was just two. Miss Carmichael is proud of Esmé's pretty, long, soft hair, which she got from her Indian father, but she doesn't like the glass eye that she also got from him. In the last school holidays, Esmé and her mother came to stay with Miss Carmichael. She had played dolly-house in the yard with Esmé. She had wished then for a real plastic dolly tea-set to play with, instead of an old milk tin and a calabash. She found it hard not to look at Esmé's glass dolly-eye while they played. "It's rude to stare at people who have something wrong with them," Mammy had cautioned.

Her dearest wish now is to get a pink dolly in a white organdie dress with puffed sleeves and a frill at the hem and red shoes and a big red waist sash and bow, and long yellow hair. The dolly would have blue glass eyes that open and close when she is lifted upright or put to lie down. A dolly is such a big, such an enormous present, that she imagines only Father Christmas could give it. If she prayed to Father Christmas, would he remember that she prayed to him for a dolly looking just like the little girl on the swing or would he get her prayers mixed up and give her instead the dolly tea-set she had prayed for?

The girl is just passing Seemungal's Variety Store, a one-door establishment. Her eyes flicker idly across to the glass display case which fronts onto the pavement. She expects to see the usual array of pencils and rulers and sharpeners and copybooks. But her breath is trapped fast behind her ribs when she sees what Seemungal has laid out today: a row of small beaded purses, pink and yellow, with patterns of flowers and leaves picked out in red and green beads. At the top, each little purse has a shiny little gold zip, pulled by a plump silky tassel, looking as soft and gleaming as an angel's wing. She does not think she has ever seen anything so exquisitely beautiful. Seemungal's lady is sitting on a stool behind the display case. The girl feels the lady's eyes pressing on her as she leans over the glass case to see the little purses more clearly.

"I tired telling allyou children to don't lean on the glass case," Seemungal's lady grumbles, in an irritated, sulky voice.

The girl steps back on to the pavement. She keeps on peering and tries again. "You could let me see one of the purses?"

"What happen? You can't see them from where you standing? You blind or what?"

If I was blind, I wouldn't be able to see what I asking you to see a little closer, she answers, but only to herself in her head. She looks at Seemungal's lady's face to check whether she could read people's minds and guesses maybe not. She peers more closely through the display case, careful now not to lean on the glass. Her fingers tingle as she imagines them running over the beads, her fingertips reading the neat, straight lines in which the tiny, perfect bead balls are arranged.

"Is how much for the purse?"

She is ashamed to hear her voice coming out so small and shaky. Seemungal's lady has picked up a grey rag and is using it to rub circles on the top of the glass display case. She is wiping the spot where the girl was leaning over. She looks intent on her task, as if something indelible would be left on the glass if she doesn't clean it at once. She doesn't look at the girl who begins to wonder whether she is invisible or made of glass herself. After a long pause, Seemungal's lady gestures with her chin towards the corner of the display case where there is a piece of paper, a torn-out piece of ruled exercise book page, with writing on it in pencil. She reads "12c." Twelve cents. That is a lot of money. She has no money of her own. Some days she gets a penny to spend at school and she spends it at once. Even if she gets a penny every school day from the following day, and does not spend any – she does a quick calculation – twelve cents is still six days' worth of pennies. She doesn't have six school days left before the party and the presents exchange. Maybe she could ask Mammy for twelve cents to buy it. But that depends on Pappy visiting and giving Mammy money. What else can she think of? Maybe if she does not go to cinema on Saturday coming and the next Saturday, Mammy could let her have twelve cents instead? But, when she goes cinema, she takes the little ones, and if she doesn't go, they can't go alone, and they wouldn't have their treat, and it would all be her fault. She steals a glance at the purses again, the pretty pink ones, the pretty yellow ones. She knows that anyone who gets that pretty pink purse, or that pretty yellow one, would be so happy. She hopes that she gets something as precious as that little purse when it is her turn to pick a present from the bag next Friday.

Seemungal's lady has sat down again. She makes a loud steups, sucking her teeth long, loud and moist, all the while tapping the heel of her sapat on the concrete floor.

"Yuh buying something or not? If yuh not buying anything stop blocking the door. It have people who want to see inside."

The girl looks around for the people who want to see inside and whom she is blocking, but sees nobody. Still, she tears herself away from the apparition of the display and continues her journey, hurrying on to Nennen Clara's yard.

Four one-room houses rise on wooden stilts above a bare beaten dirt yard. From a patch of weeds at the base of the lamppost, a vine climbs. The angled afternoon sunlight picks out dense bunches of delicate lacy coralita flowers, the same pink as the pretty little pink purse. The crinkly, heart-shaped leaves are draped in huge drooping swathes along the electric wires and over the roof and wall of a fifth precarious structure in the background. The strong smell that surrounds that building announces that it is the latrine. From it, a thin stream flows through the yard where a straggle of clean-neck and frizzle-fowl chickens strut, fluttering up against one another as if to see who is tallest. They wander about, jerking their heads forward and pecking aimlessly in the softened earth. Nennen Clara's house is the first on the left. She looks up at the doorway where a pink lace curtain hangs. She calls out, "Afternoon, Nennen, afternoon. I reach for the children."

Chubby one-year-old Tony peeps out round the curtain. He was christened Anthony after St Anthony, the saint you pray to to find lost things. Three girls born one after the other while Pappy prayed for a boy. St Anthony answered his prayers and found Tony for him. She wonders where Tony had been lost. Maybe God had a package of children for Mammy and Pappy and sent the girls down first. She wonders what would have happened if Tony had pushed himself forward and come down before she did. Would Mammy and Pappy have wanted more children or would she and Lynette and Caroline have been left behind like the time Mammy, coming home from market, left behind a bag full of ground provision that she had pushed under the seat of the bus? Mammy took another bus to the terminus but the people in charge down there said that they didn't know anything about no provision left on any bus. They said maybe the provision was found and taken away by somebody else.

Would that have happened to them, to her, if Tony had come down first? What if Mammy and Pappy didn't pray for the girls afterwards? Would she have been given to some other person? Maybe she could have been that little girl Mabel was pushing on the swing. With the golden hair and white dress with the red sash. Her own hair is black and curly. Why do some people come out looking one way and other people another way? God decides that, she knows, but how does He choose which children to put with which parents? Did you have to be specially good before you were born, when you were still in heaven with God, to be sent down with golden hair to parents who had a swing in the yard and a white dress with a red sash waiting for you? She tries to imagine a time before she was born, when she still had a chance, but she can't.

Nennen Clara comes to the doorway and Tony hides behind her dress, which hangs straight and loose from her bony frame. The girl can't tell what colour or colours the dress is because the pattern is washed out and everything is just smudges of grey. Lynette and Caroline, faces sticky and snotty from the cold that kept them from school today, shake the wooden steps as they run down to the yard while Nennen follows carrying Tony and a paper bag. She transfers Tony to the girl's left hip and puts the bag in her right hand.

"The bottle in there. It still dirty. We didn't get any water in the standpipe today. He didn't drink all the flour pap. He not himself at all today. And tell your Mammy, don't forget me Saturday."

The four set off for home past the little park. Tony is hot and heavy on her hip; his head rests on her shoulder and he has dozed off. She slides a glance across to the little tree the governor's lady-wife planted in the park the month before. A low picket fence, as high as the tree, has been put up around it. She remembers the police band playing and everybody standing stiff and still, singing "God save the King". The governor's lady-wife was wearing a black and white flowered dress with a wide white belt, white high-heeled toeless and backless shoes and a big white hat. She remembers that, at the time of the tree-planting, she had some-how got the confused idea that the governor's lady-wife was Mrs Simpson, the woman the king gave up the throne for in the old newsreels. At the planting ceremony, one of the men handed the lady a small silver shovel and she put some dirt around the roots of the little tree that another man had put down into the hole for her. The governor's lady-wife had on long white gloves reaching above her elbows.

She had never seen real gloves on a real person before. What if she pulled out a pair of long white gloves from the bran tub bag next Friday? She stifles a laugh as she imagines the ridiculous scene. People wearing gloves belonged in films, like Grace Kelly, or like the burglar or murderer in detective stories who was being careful not to leave fingerprints at the scene of the crime. In those stories, the criminal always slipped-up at the last minute – took off his right glove to light a cigarette and then move an ashtray with his bare hand or turned on a kitchen tap and picked up a glass to fill it with water. The governor's lady-wife did not take off her gloves. The girl supposes she had to keep them on to keep her hands clean. How do things like a tree or a shovel or another person's hand feel when you're wearing gloves, she wonders.

At the Chinese shop, she takes five hops bread "on trus'". "Lemind your Mammy tomollow is Fliday," Uncle Lio says as he writes something in Chinese on a small square of brown paper, the size that he uses to wrap half-cent salt, and he hooks the new paper onto the bent-up end of hanging wire, crowded with curling brown paper slips.

At home, she takes off her wide-brimmed Panama hat and hangs it over the dressing table mirror. She gets out of her dark blue school overall and her white school blouse and drapes them over the back of a chair, for tomorrow. She puts on her home-clothes: last year's outgrown school overall – short, washed-out and a little tight. She takes off her dusty watchckongs – she will blanco them later – and her socks, saved too, for the next day.

She steps with bare feet onto the cool, worn linoleum floor of the kitchen, the right-hand half of a shed behind the main house. She dips a pot of water from the galvanised bucket in the sink and rests it on the oilcloth-covered table. What colour will Mammy choose for the new linoleum and oilcloth for Christmas? She strokes the faded pattern of apples and pears on the blue oilcloth. She has read many fairytales with apples in them. She even knows what apple tastes like. Last Christmas Mammy bought four red ones. She sliced and shared them among the children, one apple a day for four days. She has never seen a real pear nor read any stories about one, except in the carol about a partridge in a pear tree. One card that came last Christmas had the whole song printed on it. She learnt the words by heart and could sing along whenever Rediffusion Radio played it. The card had a picture of a small tree with a bird on top and one pear dangling from a branch below. The pear and the bird were outlined in gold. Where did they get a pen with gold ink? Is there really such a thing as gold ink? Which would she rather have, gold ink or a little pink purse or maybe even a real pear?

She looks at her right hand, index and middle fingers stained at the last joint where they touch. School ink is blue-black, poured each morning by the monitor into white porcelain ink-wells set into exactly-the-right-size holes that punctuate the grooves in the tops of the long desk-and-bench furniture shared by half a dozen little girls. The ink does not wash off easily and the smudges last through the weekend, marring her otherwise pristine Sunday-best appearance at Mass and Sunday school, to be refreshed on Monday morning. Mammy says it's a good thing the uniform is dark blue because she can't imagine how she manages to get the ink on her skirt, too. The girl hasn't confessed that, when the nib catches on a long, blue-black ink clot fished from the bottom of the inkwell, she wipes the pen in her skirt, and not on the tightly rationed pink blotting paper that sits in the class stationery cupboard. She doesn't know how she got to be so untidy. It adds to Mammy's problems and she wishes she could be neater, like Uncle Lio's daughters. When they come home, their overalls are as clean and as sharply pleated as when they stepped out of the shop in the morning.

She tiptoes to reach the box of matches on the ledge next to the bottle of salt. She lights one burner of the three-burner pitch-oil stove and sets the pot to boil. She opens the door of the wire-sided food safe and takes out the tin of Fry's cocoa and the saucer of water with the tin of condensed milk sitting in it and rests them on the table. Four red ants are floating in the water. How do they pass through the fine mesh, she wonders, as she dips them out with a finger, wiping dry the damp finger on her skirt. She measures out one big spoon of cocoa powder, tips the spoon over into the big white jug, then pours three big spoons of condensed milk, cutting off the thick stream with a finger, which she licks clean. She puts the cocoa tin back into the safe and closes the door. She takes four cups from the top of the safe. They are real breakable cups with pictures of pink roses and green leaves on their sides. She likes to run her fingers over the surface of these cups. Mammy had bought them as a present to herself and the children. Mammy can't bring herself to use the enamel cups that everybody else uses. "They get chip-up too quick," she says, "and then the rims get rough and look nasty." The girl thinks again about the little pink and yellow purses at Seemungal's. She likes pretty things too, like Mammy, she decides.

When the water is bubbling she pours it into the jug and stirs. She pours out four cupfuls of cocoa tea and leaves them on the table to cool. There is enough left in the jug for Mammy when she comes home. She peels the shrivelled pieces of banana leaf off the top of two of the hops bread, tears open the loaves, and pours condensed milk from the tin on the four halves. She adds a little water to the saucer and puts the milk tin back into the safe. She hands the little ones each a cupful of cocoa tea and half-a-hops-bread-with-condensed-milk right where they are sitting on the back steps. They all sit there having their supper as they wait for Mammy to come home from work. She can hardly wait to tell Mammy the news about the party and about the little purses at Seemungal's.

When Mammy pushes open the back gate, she looks tired, but, when sees the four children sitting on the steps, her smile comes on, lifting up the creases at the corners of her mouth. She comes over to share hugs, but when she picks up Tony to put him on her lap she says, "He feeling hot, like he has fever." She touches the girl's head. "Go pick some chandelier and make a tisane for him." The girl leaves her bread and cocoa on the step, finds the chandelier bush in back yard, picks some leaves and puts them to boil with a cupful of water and a heaped spoonful of brown sugar. She passes the pale greeny-brown brew and a spoon to Mammy, now sitting, rocking from side to side and hugging the little ones on the back step. Mammy feeds Tony spoonfuls of the hot bitter tea, blowing on each spoonful to cool it. She is still wearing her work clothes: the white uniform of the kitchen staff at the mental hospital. Her forehead is wrinkled at the top of her nose and the creases that run down its sides are now even more deeply grooved than when she came home. "Take the towel and wet a corner in the bucket, then wipe Lynette and Caroline's faces. Make them blow their noses properly. I don't want that cold to get any worse." Tony starts whimpering peevishly, pushing away the cup of tisane; Mammy coaxes him a little, then sighs, exhaling a low desperate whisper, "Lord, put a hand."

The girl hears the faint plea as she returns to her bread and cocoa. If the Lord listens to Mammy and does decide to put a hand, the first thing He would do is put His hand over her mouth to prevent her from saying anything to Mammy about anything, just in case she can't control what she says and *mouth open, story jump out*. She sits quietly on the step. She eats her bread. She drinks her cocoa. She brushes the crumbs from her skirt as she rises to collect the empty cups from the little ones. She goes to the kitchen and pours the last of the cocoa into a cup and brings it out to Mammy. She bites her lips together as she touches the top of Mammy's head and when Mammy looks up, the girl hands over the cup.

The girl lifts Tony on to her hip and walks with him out the gate to the corner. She hugs him, sways him on her hip, tries to distract him from his whimpering while they listen to the shrieks of neighbourhood children bringing to a close their street games as their mothers hurry them indoors. She stands and listens to the cheerful hailing out of grown-ups walking home from work with the darkness coming on. She knows, she understands, that she can't tell Mammy about the class party, the exchange of presents, and the little yellow and pink purses at Seemungal's. Not tonight. She turns to go back to her yard. She looks down at the pavement, careful about where she is putting her bare feet. *Step on a crack, break your mother's back*. Maybe, tomorrow will be better.

THE DAY THE EARTH STOOD STILL

The main news item on the radio was about a girl of nine and her mother's still-hot flatiron. My sister and I, immersed in a dolly-house game, heard it over the neighbour's Rediffusion turned full blast to share with the whole yard. The announcer's words, telling the unthinkable, froze the moment. Lynette halted the little pink plastic teapot in mid-pour; my cup stopped halfway between saucer and lips; the breeze held the coconut palm branches in their up-sway, spiky leaves like flashing swords; the Plymouth Rock hen stilled in mid neck-stretch over a paralysed congaree. Then, my younger sister's eyes lifted from the teapot into my waiting eyes. We didn't speak about it but we had reason to remember that news item the following Saturday.

Lynette and I went with the neighbourhood children to our regular double-feature, twelve-thirty show at Olympic Theatre. That Saturday the main feature was *The Day the Earth Stood Still*. We sat in the darkness of the hot, airless cinema completely absorbed in the action on the shimmering screen, and even after the doors were opened at the end and we emerged, blinded by the sharp, white, afternoon light, we still hadn't left the world of the film. On the way home we relived it, acting out the scene in the elevator and its panicky aftermath when the star boy, an alien disguised as an earthling, pushed a button and shut down all the power stations in the world. "*Klaatu barada nikto!*" we chorused, saving the world from annihilation. The other children hived off as we passed their yards and soon we entered ours, walking round the house to the two back rooms where our family lived.

As we passed under the open window I could hear my little brother whimpering, but otherwise there was silence. I wondered why Mammy hadn't picked him up to comfort him. When

I got to our door, facing on to the common backyard, I saw our neighbour, with whom we shared the house, sitting on her steps with a bowl in her lap. She turned her head towards me, glanced in that low, cut-eye way at the level of my shoes and turned back to shelling peas, dropping them into her bowl in a deliberate gesture as if that action was for the record. Her daughter, a girl of twelve like me, was standing in their doorway. She didn't look my way. She was studying her bare feet like they were a subject for exams. Even though the neighbour and her daughter seemed to be busy with their own business, I felt that it was me that they were really paying attention to. It was like I was in a drama and I had just come on stage, and they were spectators waiting to see what the character I was playing would do. I felt my face and hands go clammy.

I stood in the doorway and at first wondered why there was a bundle of clothes on the floor and why my baby brother was mewling and rocking his body against it. I went in closer and saw that the bundle was Mammy, lying on her side, drawn up in a ball, her face turned away from the door. I knelt beside Junior and peered over. She was lying on her folded left arm, her face buried in its crook. Her other arm, her right arm, was hanging down, bent in a peculiar way. As I leaned against her I tried to feel for the rise and fall of her chest, but I wasn't sure whether what I could detect was her breathing or mine. I wondered whether she had fainted, as children sometimes did in school, but I had never known Mammy to faint. I shook her shoulder but she didn't move, didn't make a sound. I shook her again and again, harder and harder. I didn't know what else to do. I tried to call out, to call her name. I couldn't. I opened my mouth but my throat had closed off, something had stoppered the voice in me, shutting it off. All I had was a coldness in me and a need to shake and shake my mother, to make her wake up, to move, to say something, to make her aware of me. I rocked her shoulder back and forth until I heard, coming from far down in her chest, a noise, a deep, hoarse, "Uhgggn… uhgggn…" like a hurt creature, and with that noise, some of the heavy coldness in my body lifted away, for then I knew for sure that the thought I hadn't allowed myself to think was not the reality.

She made that awful animal noise again as she squirmed her head slowly out of the crook of her arm and turned so I could see her face. It was not a face I knew. It was like a face from a scary film. Her eyes were puffed up and all around them was grey and puffed up too. One cheek was swollen, a thin trickle of blood streaked from a nostril and made little puddles in the tiny basins of her pores. Her mouth hung down, her lips were parted and I could see her top gums showing raw, red pits at the front. This face didn't look like my mother's. I pulled back from her and pulled Junior away too.

It was then that my eye caught the small figure wedged in a corner. My littlest sister was sitting on the floor, staring straight ahead. I lifted my brother and went over to her. She was sitting in a wet patch and she didn't seem to know that, or to know me. I touched the top of her head.

"Noelle, what happen?"

She didn't answer. I bent over, putting Junior on the floor next to her. He put his head on her shoulder. She looked up at me.

"Noelle, tell me what happen."

She looked down at her hands, twisting, fighting each other in her lap. I held her hands still, stooping to catch her whisper, "Pappy come."

Lynette had not moved from the doorway. I motioned her towards me. She walked stiffly, like she was a robot, looking ahead but not seeing or hearing anything. I held her face in my hand and shook it. Her eyes focused on me and I could see she was on the edge of crying. I said, "Don't start any of that crying foolishness. You have to behave like a big girl." I went over to Mammy.

"Mammy, try to sit up."

Mammy struggled hard to lean on her left arm to raise her upper body. I pushed at her back, helping her to roll forward, to be more sitting than lying. She was hanging down her head so I couldn't see her face, only her crown, where pale scalp showed through her fine, thin hair clotted into dark clumps. I stood there not knowing what to do next. I had never been responsible for an injured person before and I had no lessons in first-aid to guide me. But I had read enough books and comics and seen enough films to have some pattern to follow. Somehow I got hold of myself and at first behaved as if I was following a manual. There was a cup on the table; I picked it up and went outside to the pipe in the kitchen shed. I filled it and brought it to her.

"Here, drink some water."

She took the cup and brought it to her lips. A drop of blood dripped from her nose into the water as she put her lips to the rim but she didn't notice. She sipped a little and, wincing, handed back the cup. We didn't say anything to each other and I wondered what to do next. The two little ones in the corner started crying, not loudly, but it was more than I could deal with and I snapped at them.

"Stop that right now; you making it worse."

They looked up, shocked, stopped crying, then hid their faces in each other's shoulders. I took the enamel basin from under the bed and sent Lynette outside to the kitchen pipe, to collect water. She brought it back a couple of inches deep. I set the basin on the floor next to our mother.

"Try to wash your face"

Mammy leaned over the basin and cupped water in her left hand, splashing her face. Little swirls of red fading to pink filtered through the clear water, but her face was still patchy with clots. She wasn't very good with her left hand and the floor got splashed too. I took an outgrown, outworn school blouse destined to become rags and bit through the end of the fabric to help with tearing a piece off. I passed the rag to her. Mammy dipped it into the water and did a more thorough job on her face.

"Here," I handed back the cup, "rinse out your mouth."

She did as I said, spitting into the basin. The water turned red.

I took the basin and rag outside, emptied the water into the drain, rinsed out the rag, squeezed it, refilled the basin and went back inside. She was sitting up better this time, but still on the floor. Now that I could see her face, it seemed to me that it was worse than when it was bloodstained, because I could see each part separately, like evidence in a detective story: shifted nose, broken lips, missing teeth, cut cheekbone, gashed temple, bruised eyes. And there was that right arm hanging down crooked, that she wouldn't let me touch. I had never seen her as bad as this after one of Pappy's visits. What should I do next? I had done as much as I could and I didn't know if what I had done was the right thing. I felt that it was all more than I could bear. Why was life like this? Why was life something that happened to you and you didn't know how or why or what; you in a constant state of not knowing? Not knowing what to do when something happens to you that is bigger than you and you are the biggest person around and you have to do something, and what you do must be the right thing. I didn't know whether to ask a neighbour for help, or whether to go down the road to use the phone in the shop. And to call whom? Police? Ambulance? Who would help? I thought about that and remembered that when the neighbour was having a baby, she sent for the nurse who lived nearby.

"I am going up the road for Nurse Brooks to look at that arm."

Nurse Brooks, the official neighbourhood midwife and, as I was to discover years later, unofficial abortionist, came with me wearing her on-duty white uniform. She was bearing her big black bag, the one that we children believed she delivered the babies in. We helped Mammy to a chair near the table and I stood beside her as Nurse Brooks told me what to do. She rested Mammy's arm on the table and I held the upper arm tight as Nurse Brooks pulled the lower arm. Mammy was by now white and limp and cold and damp; she squeezed her lips tight shut, squeezed her eyes tight shut, would not shame herself by making noise, would not cry, would not let her business go outside. When the broken bone ends were lined up to her satisfaction, Nurse Brooks laid two wooden school rulers along the arm, one above, one underneath, wrapped around an elastic bandage and pinned it in place. She took one of Junior's diapers and made a sling.

"That will do for now but you have to go to the hospital and get a plaster-of-Paris cast put on that arm… for the latest tomorrow. Let me deal with your face now."

She splashed a capful of Dettol into the basin of water, clouding it white, dipped the rag and cleaned the injuries. Mammy didn't protest as Nurse Brooks dabbed the Dettol solution into her cuts and I know it must've stung a lot. Maybe the pain in her arm had made the other pain slight in comparison. When she was done, Nurse Brooks sent me out to the sink to wash the basin and when I got back I realised that she and Mammy had been talking about what had happened.

As she was making to leave, she said, "You women have to learn to stop provoking your men. If they have rules, stick by the rules. What you expect when you break rules, eh? Punishment."

After she left, I sat by Mammy's side on the floor and wanted to ask her what she had been punished for. I wanted to know what had she done to make him to act like this. This was not the first time he had beaten her; what did she do to make him do this to her again and again? Did we children have anything to do with whatever was going on between these big people? Was it our fault? None of us ever spoke about it, even Lynette and me, we bigger children. It was just something that happened, that you put up with because you had no understanding and no control. It wasn't different from other things I didn't understand like earthquake, flood or fire. Even licks in school was not different from man beating woman, or even death, which could come to anybody at any time. But this time I wanted to know about us, about what caused sudden calamity in our family. I looked up at Mammy, still seated on the chair.

"What happened?"

Her answer dripped from between her swollen lips, like feeble drops struggling from the tap when water has been shut off.

"I let you… go… theatre… without… asking him… first."

"But we always go twelve-thirty on Saturday."

"He don't know that. He just happen to come here today and see the two of you missing."

"And just for that, he do you this?"

She dropped her head.

"What he hit you with?"

She looked away, not saying.

"Why you didn't hit him back?"

She looked down at me, puzzled.

"He would've killed me. He would've killed Noelle and Junior too."

"Why you don't just leave him? We should just leave him."

She looked down as her breath came out in a long, worn-out, draining sighs.

"And who will mind the four of you? Where we will live? My mother dead, father dead, sisters and brothers have their own troubles."

She waited for this to sink in, then went on, even more resignedly.

"You just too young to understand life."

If this was the life I was to understand, I didn't want to. I stood up and shouted.

"I will kill him. You hear me? I will kill him."

"You don't know what you saying. You want to get hanged for murder?"

"I don't care. And too besides, they don't hang children."

"Don't talk like that. Something must've got him vexed in the club and he came down here to take out his vexation. He was drinking. He was too drunk to know what he was doing."

"He will soon find out. Let him come back here. Then he will know what he was doing."

Big talk, stargirl talk, I knew Mammy was thinking. Maybe it was bravado, but I didn't want to be part of any of this. I couldn't bear the weight of this heavy life any more.

"Instead of going up the road for Nurse Brooks, I should have gone by the police station for him."

"You think the police would have listened to you? A child making a complaint about her father?"

"But what he did is called assault. It's against the law."

"Child, they would say that that is man and woman business, and send you straight back home."

"So, he can come back anytime he wants and do this again?"

"Men feel that because they minding you they have a perfect right to do what they want to you. You are only a child. You can't change that."

In truth, that was how it was. Those were the real rules, there to keep us in check. Still, there had been times, more often perhaps recently, when we had strayed out from under the edges of his control, not always behaving as we were expected to. We had friends we knew he could not approve of, went places without his knowledge. It was as if we had, with Mammy's tacit sanction, decided to do what we wanted to do when he wasn't present. After all, we hardly saw him, and we would only behave in the way he expected of us when he was there, seeing us. We never talked about it. It was just the way we worked around and through what life had given us, given all of us, including Mammy. Now that glimpse of freedom seemed under threat.

We spent the next few hours in a kind of nothing way. I gave the children hops bread with some guava jelly that Mammy had made just the day before. The jelly was clear and red and looked like a jewel, and normally I would have put a big spoonful in my mouth and savoured its tart sweetness, but that day I couldn't eat it. I had seen enough red.

Later, we were sitting silent on the back steps cooling down in the evening breeze when the neighbour's daughter ran through their part of the house, down their back step, into the shared kitchen. Her whisper was loud enough for us children to hear.

"Ma, it look like he come back."

Through my head ran the weary knowledge that you've got to be lucky to *see* him arrive as no one ever *hears* him arrive. You'd be doing something somewhere in the house or yard and suddenly you'd feel uncomfortable, aware of a watching presence, or you'd glance sidelong on the floor and see a pair of brown lace-up leather shoes leading up to brown socks and brown pants, or a long dark shadow would fall over your etched-in-the-red-dirt circle of marbles, or hopscotch squares and you'd look up and he'd be there and you'd have no idea how long he'd been present or how much of what you were doing he'd seen, and you'd wonder whether what you were doing was wrong, something he didn't approve of.

He must've realised he had been spotted that evening because he did not enter by the front gate. He came through the lane at the side of the house and opened the back gate. We saw him at once from the back steps where we had drawn close, huddling together at the news of his arrival. I thought he was a little taken aback to find us there, all present and correct, because he slowed down and seemed a little unsure. But he quickly regained his rhythm and walked towards the seated group.

"I see all you reach back. Where all you was?"

His voice was low. Not loud enough that the neighbours could

46

hear what he was saying, but we heard. No one answered. Neither Lynette nor I looked up to meet his eyes.

"Who tell you that you could go matinee, eh? Who in charge here? Me or you?"

I felt the menace in his words lash me about my bowed head. I knew who was in charge, but I just couldn't lift my head to say, *you, Pappy, you in charge.*

"You feel you is big woman to do what you want? If you is big woman, why you don't go and get man to mind you? Don't look for me to give all you mother money every week to mind you."

Perhaps it was our silence, our obvious helplessness, perhaps it was whatever had got him angry, maybe at the club earlier, perhaps it was seeing how badly he had injured Mammy this time, that made him go in a direction he hadn't gone before, maybe he was trying to prove to himself, and to everybody, that he was right to do what he had done. For, why else would he tell his little girls of twelve and nine they should turn to finding men to support them if he stopped giving Mammy money? No one in our family would ever say a thing like that. No one would even have a thought like that. It was as if he had brought us a new way of thinking about ourselves. A very shocking way of thinking that was about a kind of people we didn't know, who weren't friends or neighbours, had a different kind of life from ours. Mammy's head bent lower. The little ones looked frightened. Noelle started to snivel and Junior joined in. Lynette's voice came out cracked, but angry.

"The little children didn't do you anything. Why you making them cry for?"

"But look at my crosses! Who you think you is to tell me what to do? You forgetting your place. I will have to remind you who is the boss here. Like is your turn to learn a lesson today, my girl."

In slow motion, drawing out each action as he looked steadily at her, he eased the end of his belt from its loop, folded it back at the buckle and slid the pin from the hole. We were all staring at what he was doing, transfixed. We children, at least we older ones who could understand what was happening, were never present when he beat Mammy; it was always in private, between him and her, and we didn't know what triggered his rages. We would come home and find her bruised and bleeding, but we were never witnesses. But while this action of his was not familiar to us, we understood what it meant. He grasped the heavy buckle in his right hand, drawing the belt through the loops of his pants waist. He folded the belt in half, grasping the buckle and the loose end. He had never hit one of us children before and he was about to beat Lynette. Nothing was like anything I had known before.

A bright image filled my whole mind. It was of that little nine-year-old girl going to the coalpot where the charcoal still glowed red, taking up a thick cloth to grip the handle of her mother's hot flatiron resting there, raising up that flatiron over her head and bringing it down on to her sleeping father's head. The dazzling light blinded out all other thought, burning away my ability to think. *Klaatu barada nikto!* I had to stop him. Not fully conscious of what I was doing, I leaned over, picked up a stone, and pelted it at the side of his head. He must've caught the movement from the corner of an eye, because at that instant he turned his head and the stone struck his left eye. His hands dropped the belt and flew up to his face. It was as if a spell had been broken. Lynette, seizing his distracted moment, grabbed a piece of brick and hurled it at the other side of his face. Blood was trickling from the eye, and the cheek, where the brick fragment had struck, was already swelling. The yard neighbours moved closer for a better view. Mammy stood up, walked towards him, her crude sling like a shield before her. She bent down, picked up the belt from the ground, handed it to him, looked him straight in his eyes and said, "Go!"

I NEVER HEARD PAPPY PLAY THE HAWAIIAN GUITAR

I never heard Pappy play the Hawaiian guitar, an experience they say caused big, hardback men to halt at the crunch of a hang-jack moment in an all-fours card game, jaded women to rise from the fumbling laps of drink-sotted men, and broken-nosed barmen to pause in their rinsing of glasses in basins of grey water. This was in those wrought-iron-balconied upstairs places facing the docks along South Quay where he and his Hawaiian guitar spent whole unbroken weekends after he had pocketed his tally-clerk pay envelope on Saturday mornings.

But then, there was a whole lot I didn't know about Pappy. Where he lived, whom he lived with, what he liked, or didn't, were just a few of the mysteries of my childhood, so, when I heard him eulogised at his funeral service, thirty-one years ago today, as the finest player of the Hawaiian guitar in town, I was both surprised and not at all surprised. It wasn't that I didn't know anything about Pappy, it's just that what I did know was gleaned solely through sparse but careful observation, knowledge from the tiniest seeds of clues scattered around my world. Some of the things I knew first hand. The domestic control he exercised over us even while seldom present in person didn't help me to judge him in a balanced way when I was a child, but today I'm not going to weigh and measure him. I guess the Almighty or maybe St Peter did the plusses and minuses of Pappy's life long years ago as he approached the judgement seat, brown fedora in hand, seeking the final verdict on his sixty-eight years. I'd put my money on St Peter doing the job. I don't think Pappy would've warranted a personal audience with the Almighty, with whom he had been conflated in my mind in my very early years, any more than he would have been known as an individual human being by his august employer, Mr Kennedy, of Wm Kennedy & Co Import and Export who, I suppose, was like a god in the universe of Pappy's work.

Pappy's job at Kennedy's was to go on the docks when the ships came in and to check the company's landed cargo and also do the same for cargo going out – import and export. I never saw what came in. We girls were screened from contact with that world where, it was reported, women tossed back their heads and laughed loudly with men who whistled and called out to them – the men guiding the massive rope-wrapped pallets swinging from cranes on the ships lying alongside, down to the dockside. But I did have a first-hand knowledge of what went out since I was often at the Kennedy & Co warehouse. As the eldest, it fell to me to go to Pappy's workplace on Saturdays, to seek him out and wheedle him into sending some of the contents of his pay envelope back to Mammy, who would be waiting at home in Belmont, anxiously calculating in her head how the hoped-for fifteen dollars could be spread among her string of waiting creditors, to keep all reasonably happy and in check for the coming week.

Dressed-up in last Easter's church dress, I boarded the bus as it moved sedately through quiet, residential Belmont and disembarked on lower Charlotte Street, just where the bus sputtered to a crawl, edging its cautious way through the Central Market's overflow of vendors and their fruit and vegetables, fish and flesh – the perfume of ripe pineapple and the stench of hot animal blood mingling in a single intake of breath. I sauntered along Marine Square, so fascinated by the busyness of commercial life that I lost all sense of purpose and allowed the tide of swaying women, who balanced on their heads big, round split-bamboo baskets perched on twists of cloth, and men, who transported handcarts of boxes of goods from wholesalers to retailers, to sweep me along at their pace. I stopped to touch pavement displays of combs – family-sized, clear plastic amber ones with dark flecks trapped inside, two-sided small silver metal ones for combing out lice, small black ones for fitting in men's shirt pockets. I had to sidestep the beggars, women with cupped hands extended, squatting on the pavement, long skirts drooping in modesty between their knees, faces half-hidden by thin ohrinis draped across their noses from which hung large silver filigree nose rings, and men who were ratty-bearded and ragged, bare-footed and dirty, downcast and aggressive, subdued and loud. Everything grabbed attention – enamel cups in beige and white with blue rims, ballpoint pens that could write in three colours of ink with the slide of a knob, four-stacked metal food carriers craftily held together by rods slotted into their handles, black and white knitted alpagatas threaded with patterns of red and green wool. All this, and more, overlaid by a cacophony of sound – loud calls competing with clanging bicycle bells, the abrupt blare of car horns and the raucous shouts of donkey cart drivers.

As I passed the Cathedral of the Immaculate Conception, I made sure to make the Sign of the Cross across my chest, to invoke good fortune in my quest. I strayed and delayed my unwilling arrival at my destination. From the bright white glare of the pavement, I peered through the deep shade of the over-hanging upper-floor balcony into the even darker interior. For a long while I could make out nothing, then jute-brown crocus bags emerged in soft focus in serried ranks, wooden pillars rose to support the storey above and I could just pick out, way in the back, a platform on which was a wooden desk, a chair and a man's pale face, like a misplaced moon, floating above a khaki shirt. This man was the first of those I was dressed to impress on Saturdays. "Yuh looking for yuh fadda?" he called out, and I nodded in embarrassed agreement. He then turned his face to make a last quarter phase to shout into the darker recesses, "Jimmy still there?" At this I stopped breathing, crossed my fingers and said a silent prayer, for if I was late, late through dawdling, and if the answer came, *No, Jimmy done gone already*, indicating that Pappy had picked up his pay and left, that would be a disaster for us for the coming week, and how would I explain to Mammy why I had failed to do what she had sent me to do?

But not this time. For today, just today, I will remember Pappy still being there and him coming from that back space where he was doing whatever mysterious thing that tally-clerks do when not on the docks. He is moving slowly and fluidly towards me,

51

wiping his hands with a white handkerchief that he is looking at intently, not pausing as he folds it first in half, then in quarters, into a neat, deliberate square, edges and corners perfectly aligned, then folding over a corner to meet the opposite one, making a fat triangle that he pats and flattens and is already placing, with a straight palm to avoid it creasing, into a back pocket, by the time he gets to me. He is bending over for me to plant an unwilling but dutiful peck on his cheek, the sickly scent of tobacco rising from his pores cancelling out, for that moment, the pervasive, unidentifiable dusty smells of that gloomy cavern. We stand facing each other, each waiting for the other to say something first.

"Mammy send me for the money." I, unschooled in tact and diplomacy, break the spell.

"And yuh wouldn't come to look for yuh fadder otherwise?" he challenges.

For years and years, I replayed that scene, just so – setting: the warehouse; characters: father and girlchild; situation: girlchild requesting child-support from father – and I wonder today whether I had been too simplistic, too judgemental in my reading of him all those many, painful Saturdays of long ago. In that scene of the past, it isn't just Pappy and me there. Standing there with us, in us, were the people we thought we were, and the people we thought we should be. I was girlchild, yes, but also convent-girl, and so I was divided between two worlds – the one that contained the expectations and standards of the chaste world of Irish nuns and their ideal students, my French-creole, plantation-owning and merchant-class schoolmates, and the less privileged underworld of my own real life. As to Pappy – at work he was tally-clerk, at home, rarely visiting father, and there was also a secret life that none of us at home was privy to. Now I see that when Pappy and I encountered each other on Saturday mornings, we were in the gladiatorial arena of malehood in the mid-twentieth century when role models were Jack Palance, Humphrey Bogart and John Wayne. So when Pappy was walking towards me, he was walking towards a camera from a long shot. He had a role to play, that while moving to a tight close-up, he was trying to show that he is Man. He is Man, to be recognized as such by a visible and invisible audience and maybe, above all, by himself.

But back then, as I stood within the warehouse of Wm H Kennedy and Sons, Marine Square, Port of Spain, I understood nothing, only that my mother had sent me to my father and I was being deflected by his challenge that I wouldn't come to see him if it were not to get money from him. It was a challenge I couldn't take up because it had a shape and size and facets and angles beyond my comprehension and I didn't know how to deal with it at any level – joking or serious, as stated or as implied. I hung my head, ashamed that it was indeed so, that I wouldn't come to look for my father unless I had been sent for money, and that he had drawn that shameful ingratitude of mine and of the whole tribe of us dependants to the attention of his watching and listening audience of fellow-men, who themselves had women and children to contend with.

Pappy throws off that pose and takes on the responsible, proud father one saying, "Come over here and say good morning to Mr. De Four." That is the moonface's name, Manuel De Four, and he is intent on spiking squares and rectangles of paper to a board of protruding nails behind his desk. I say, "Good Morning, Mr. De Four." And he, pausing in his rhythmic paper spiking, says, "So what happen, you get too big to call me Uncle Mannie now? Come and give me a kiss, chile." Chile tiptoes and leans forward to brush the roughly shaved cheek with her lips, and she can't wait to surreptitiously turn her head and with seeming casualness wipe said lips against the stiff green organdie of her puff-sleeved arm. Pappy calls out to the back darkness, "All yuh come out here and see mih daughter." Pepsi-Joe and Sonny shuffle out and one says, "But she getting big, eh Jimmy," and the other asks, "So this is the bright one?" and Mr. De Four calls over, "She must be get the good looks and the brains from the mudda," and they all laugh at this familiar joke that big people are always making on one another.

Putting his arm around my shoulders, Pappy pulls me to him. My face is against his scratchy, brown serge pants and I move closer in so as not to face the gaze of the men, because I am ashamed under scrutiny. I suspect that they are saying something else under those words and I can't guess at its hidden meaning, and I'm not sure who, if anyone, is supposed to answer. Their heh-heh-heh fades as Pepsi-Joe and Sonny disappear, back into the dim interior of the warehouse, Mr De Four resumes his paper-spiking and Pappy moves me towards the rows of sacks, his arm still around my shoulders, my two steps matching his one.

At the first row, he rolls over the loose sacking at the top of the nearest bag. At that slight disturbance, a mustiness dislodges from the sack. My hand reaches in and I take a handful of large seeds, dull, rough ovals and I close my fist and rub the contents together and as the full fragrance bursts out, I put my nose deep into my palm and inhale an intoxicating mystery, something like vanilla, but a vanilla that has journeyed through deep forests, dank leaves, slithering life, absorbing darkness, moisture, heat, decay along the way, complicating its innocent bland sweetness. I do not know where tonka beans come from, how they grow, where they are bound, what is their use. I only drink in the beans' enigmatic essence.

I drift on to another bag, to smooth, shiny-dark beans whose cloying scent I know from comforting drinks on rainy nights: the thick, oily, welcome embrace of cacao beans. These are rubbed, squeezed and inhaled too. They leave a trace that make my palms glide frictionless along each other, silky-smooth, soothing. We move to the last row – the thrill of forbidden pleasure, an adults-only pleasure – the spiky aroma of coffee beans tickling high up in my nostrils like a sneeze that won't come. Rooted there, I bury my nose into first one handful, then another, astonished at the richness and complexity of scents and sensations that have come from such undistinguished, dull, hard scraps. Are not seeds just dropped and discarded, scattered and strewn from living trees, who carry on, year after year, producing these end-products of their more attractive floral displays? Or so my child's mind runs. I squeeze, I rub, I inhale, transported in time and space, lost in my own world of the senses.

The Cathedral tower clock calls the Angelus. Everything is suspended as the loud, metallic clang of clapper on bell rim fills the air, my head, my chest with each of its heavy strikes – bang, bang, bang, pause – four cycles of three, then a pause followed by twelve sustained strikes. The sound lingers, vibrating the air and the ear for long moments after, and as it fades, it is as if a spell has been broken and the true world has been revealed. Everything springs to life in a changed direction. The bells signal the end of the working week for Pappy and for everyone else in town and I am jolted back to Saturday in the Kennedy and Sons warehouse. Pappy is anxious to go, to meet up with the boys, to start his other life, free from duty to work and family, and I must get back home to Mammy.

We stand there together, he wanting to rush away, I wanting to detain him, for I have not yet got what I came for. But I cannot ask again. Pappy has just treated me to a little distraction for my enjoyment and I cannot bring myself to be crude and remind him of what I really came for. He gives every appearance of having forgotten why I am there. He glances at his watch. I look down on the grimy cement floor. My palms are sweating with the fear that he has indeed forgotten and I will have to say it aloud again, will have to say that I have come to visit him, my father, only to get money. Pepsi-Joe and Sonny come out of the darkness and go towards the long, stout, heavy wooden bar that slot into the iron brackets when they close the wide front doors, barricading us inside. They look towards Pappy and me, waiting. Pappy now seems to remember the purpose of my visit.

Standing an arm's length from me, he draws from a back pocket a worn leather wallet and he extracts, one by one, drawing out each note into a symphony, a five-dollar bill, pause, another five-dollar bill, longer pause, and finally, with a flourish, to the mute crash of cymbals from the soundtrack, a third five-dollar bill. He fans the three bills out, a gambler with a royal flush, and, with the faintest of nods, indicates that I should put my palm out, into which one, two, three five-dollar bills are placed flat and then folded – my hot damp fingers folded by his cool, dry ones – over the limp, many-times-used paper. I untie my handkerchief, place the notes in the middle, tie all in a double knot and loop one loose end through my waistband, knotting it securely in place. He bends his head for my parting cheek peck, I deliver, then turn and run out the doorway, leaving my father until another Saturday.

I set off along Marine Square from which life has drained, save for women, squinting in the sharp white light, spilling out the Cathedral after their Angelus devotions. As I move my palm across my face to make a Sign of the Cross in gratitude for answered prayers, the essences of the crushed seeds invade my nostrils, and I feel a strange excitement and lightness. Pappy strides off in the other direction, to the wrought-iron-balconied upstairs clubs opposite the docks on South Quay, to meet up with the boys and to play his Hawaiian guitar, to the stupefaction of hard-drinking, hard-gambling men and the adoration of soft, carefree women, reeling them in with his steel-stringed vibration, which I shall never hear.

GOLD BRACELETS

Thaïs's gold bracelets were a pair of open circles, large, thick and heavy. My earliest recollection of sensual pleasure comes from sitting on her lap and playing with the bracelets on her wrists. I would close my eyes and run my fingertips along the grooves and ridges of the fat cocoa pods into which the ends of the open circles were shaped, and then the neat rows of bumps – the goldsmith's cocoa nibs that spilled from the pods – and onto warm, smooth unadorned gold. When, as children, we begged to borrow them as essential accessories in playing "big people" with her shoes and dresses and hats, she would say, "No. Not the bracelets. They're too precious." When we pestered, she would say, as if that explained everything, "My father gave them to me for my twenty-first birthday."

I can just imagine the old Frenchman saying to her, she the eldest girl with a twin sister and two younger sisters already married, "Thaïs, it looks like you are never going to find a husband. These are for you to help yourself." It was his last gift to her before he died. So said, so done.

Expecting the fruit of her first mistake at twenty-six, she made her way into uncharted territory. I can imagine her, fidgeting from one foot to the other, shrinking inside herself, hoping no one who knew her or her family would see her as she was scrutinised, from white beret to white peep-toe slingback shoes, by the Sephardic Jewish assayer at the Y De Lima pawnshop window (on the side-street around the corner from its more respectable Frederick Street Fine Jewellery establishment). After sizing her up, maybe guessing her predicament, he screwed a magnifying glass into his right eye socket, scratched at each bracelet with a little knife, set the bracelets on a delicate balance and pronounced, "Twenty-four carat gold. I give you fifteen dollars. Is three months you have to redeem. You come back, you pay extra three dollars for interest."

She used this fabulous sum to get together the layette: light white cotton that she cut into tiny chemises and sewed and embroidered on her mother's old foot-pedal Singer; soft white cotton that she cut and sewed into diapers; white wool knitted into bootees and bonnets. The baby – me – slept hemmed in by pillows on my mother's bed in my grandmother's house, while my mother did the washing and cooking for the household. "Don't think you could lie down for nine days; nobody here to do for you," her mother, embittered by shame, would have told her.

Three years later, put out of the family home with the pending second mistake, my mother again left the bracelets with Y De Lima and rented a room in the next valley. My memories of that St. Francois Valley Road home are of a pet squirrel, which we fed bread and bananas, and of a baby sister, who was fed at my mother's bosom, screened by a muslin diaper. The third mistake, another girl, again after three years, moved us to St James, the father taking responsibility, finding a better home to rent in a nicer district. This time the bracelets were pawned for payment to a cabinet maker for a Morris set – couch, one rocking chair, one armchair and a small centre table – to complement the mahogany set of bed, wardrobe and dressing table (with round mirror and stool), an earlier parting gift from her mother.

I learnt to tell the time at that third baby's christening when the godfather, the rare owner of a watch, unravelled the mysteries of the hands and the face and the numbers (how 4 could be an hour or it could be twenty past, and a 'before' and an 'after' that gave time a malleable quality that has never left me, so that I am stranded, quaintly analogue, in today's digital now). The fourth birth, a boy – his gender brought relief to my mother and huge pride to his father, who, according to his drinking buddies, had proved himself a man at last – precipitated another move, to Boissiere. There was a final move, this time without another baby, to Belmont when I was ten. This last move put the gold bracelets in captivity for a three-burner, table-top kerosene stove to replace the coalpot, another bed for the three little ones to share and a folding canvas cot in which I, as eldest, was privileged to sleep alone.

One day, when I was thirteen or so, the neighbour's son ran into the yard waving a newspaper page. "Miss Thaïs, Miss Thaïs," he gasped, "mih mammy say to check out De Lima list and see if you have anything there." As my mother took the newspaper from him, I saw that the newspaper was shaking; in fact, all of her was shaking. "Go," she said to me, "go and bring the ticket." I climbed on the dressing-table stool and fetched down the red-velvet-lined cardboard jewellery box where she kept the ticket. She leaned against the doorway as she scanned the long rows of numbers, praying under her breath that her ticket number would not match one there, but the number for her precious gold bracelets *was* there, among the hundred or so unredeemed items offered for sale the following Saturday. I had never seen my mother so distraught. She sat on the back step, her chin resting on her hand while she gazed up at the guava tree. I do not know what she read in the tracery of its fine branches and leaves against the sky, but I was despatched to an uncle-in-law who owned a liquor store, to ask for ten dollars.

Ten dollars was a lot to ask for, even though he owned a shop. It was a week's wages for a porter humping crates, boxes and barrels of alcohol from the delivery truck to the warehouse at the back of the shop. When he asked me, "So when your mother planning to pay me back if I lend her the money?" I could only hang my head; the answer to that question was not sent as part of the request. I was spilling hot tears of shame – to have to beg in front of the boys who worked in the shop, in front of the customers buying rum at four shillings a bottle – when Uncle lifted the counter flap and pressed five two-dollar bills into my hand. My mother also asked one of her brothers, the one whose living was growing roses and selling them to flower shops, and he too parted with ten dollars. "Don't worry to pay me back," he said; "that is for the children." The last ten came in ones and twos, only from family, for she would never have wanted outside people know her business. Thirty dollars, two weeks' worth of her grocery-cashier wages, went to redeem the bracelets. I was old enough and bold enough to ask, "Mammie, how you going to pay

59

it back?" and to bear witness to the answer she gave to any and all of life's uncertainties, "The Lord will provide." The Lord provided for weeks on end a bountiful harvest of guavas. Thaïs armed us children with enamel basins and packed us off to pick up the fallen fruit before the swarming fruit flies could hasten their deliquescence. She stood night after night over steaming pots of boiling fruit, adding sugar to the strained liquid, then skimming and stirring and testing and pouring out jar after jar of clear ruby jelly, and it was with gifts of this that she repaid her creditors.

I learnt that the gold bracelets sliding up and down her busy arms were my mother's insurance against the future. If the bracelets were not on her arms, they were at Y De Lima's. If I saw her leaving the house on a Saturday morning in the August school holiday and she wasn't wearing her bracelets, I knew she wouldn't be wearing them for a while yet. After the exchange at the pawnbroker's, she would be going straight to Waterman's and Glendenning's for school uniform material, and with booklists to Muir Marshall and Stephen & Todd's.

She would shop until the money almost ran out and then, laden with packages, she would go to Eden's flower shop and get some long-stemmed gladioli wrapped in a cone of translucent white paper, and then walk up to Holsum's Patisserie on Park Street to choose cream horns, custard slices, cream cakes and soupees delicately placed in a small white cardboard box, and with the string looped through an index finger, she would get in a six-cents-a-ride taxi to return home to Belmont, triumphant. (I would be in my fifties before I could understand, and so forgive, the extravagance of those blooms and pastries; but I could never match that display of faith in the present or future.)

A sou-sou running in September and October briefly released the bracelets but they were back into De Lima's in late November – for patterned cretonne for cushion covers for the Morris chairs, for lace curtains, for new linoleum for the kitchen floor and new oilcloth for the table. Basic foodstuff was always taken on trust from the Chinese shop opposite, but the big food items for Christmas, the salt ham and the chicken, the dried fruit, rum and wine for the Christmas cake were bought on Charlotte Street from a bigger grocery and these were bought cash with an early hand in a November and December sou-sou – as was the five-foot Scots pine Christmas tree at a dollar a foot, brought home in a taxi for which Thaïs always paid for two seats, on Christmas Eve. The tree stood in a bucket filled with stones and water, yet it died, slowly, shedding its sharp leaves, which years later I learned to call "needles". It filled the house with a bewildering, alien, sharp, medicinal fragrance. (I met that scent in its natural habitat for the first time walking through the Forestry Commission's rows of pines when I lived in Wales in my twenties, and every time I found myself in a pine forest thereafter, I would be taken back to my mother, without her bracelets on Christmas Day.)

Confirmation and first communion dresses, shoes, white prayer books, veils and candles with the gilt cross and lily motif; ice-cream and cake parties with neighbours at these events – all happened at the right time thanks to the gold bracelets. There was always money for church collection at Sunday Mass and small spending money for school and for the Olympic Cinema twelve-thirty double feature on Saturdays. I could never recall my mother using the phrase "cannot afford". It would have made her ashamed to even think that there was something she couldn't do for her children.

The unknown future that saw the bracelets missing in action included things like Thaïs's hysterectomy when I was eleven, Noelle's broken arm and appendicitis, Lynette's dental visit for "riders" (never corrected), and fillings for me when I was fourteen. (There were, though, not enough doctors' visits for Tony's recurring ear infections – he would need a hearing aid at forty.)

When I was twelve, someone told my mother about a house to rent for the August holidays in Toco. Thaïs loved the sea; after a sea-bath in nearby Carenage, she would let the salt dry on her skin and go to sleep without a freshwater bath. "Medicinal properties," she claimed. Excited at the idea of a seaside holiday for her children, she contacted the owner of the house and arranged to rent it for four weeks in the school holidays. It was one of three, set in a loose cluster at Trois Roches, and that first venture started the family tradition of August holidays in Toco.

I remember the packing of cardboard boxes of clothes, food items, matches, and candles for "spending time by the sea" as these holidays were called. The blue house, up on a hill, was at the eighteen and a quarter mile post. (The location, the bend in the road, the shape of the hill, the cliff on the other side of the road is deeply engraved in my memory, but I searched in vain for the blue house on every trip up that coast in the following years of my adult life).

The cycle of daily life at the Trois Roches house stays in my dreams. Mornings, off to the sea. A short climb down the cliff and on to the narrow beige sand strip and a leap into clear foamy Caribbean water. This is where we all learnt to swim, by surviving the waves and currents of the little bay with the three large black rocks sticking out of the water. Lunch back at the house, a quiet time, and then back to the sea. Later, as the sun was about to set, Thaïs would look across the bay for the sight of the sails of returning pirogues and, skins still sticky with the residue of drying seawater, we would take a steady walk down to the village, past the church at Mission and on to the fish depot. Here my mother would choose a red fish or a king fish (head and tail for the night's broth; slices fried or steamed for lunch next day) and, with the scaled and gutted trophy, we would set off back to the house, counting off the quarter-mile-posts along the black tar road.

At night, the gas lamps made a hissing noise like a den of dragons snoring. The lamps attracted thousands of suicidal rainflies. They smashed into the lights, the walls, the furniture; they collapsed into the fish broth, the cocoa tea, the bread and butter; their grey translucent wings collected in drifts in corners; their black wriggling bodies crawled aimlessly across the floor. The next morning's sweepings left a rug of squirming black and grey out the back door. (It was years later that I understood that these rainflies are termites and that the little blue house on the hill was but one stage in the process of a gentle continuous recycling of material by these tiny, purposeful creatures).

Through September the gold bracelets languished at De Lima's awaiting their release by a sou-sou hand in late October and a brief appearance on Thaïs's arms before their annual Christmas captivity. It was Thaïs's dream to be, one day, actually wearing her bracelets for Christmas. That did not happen until many years had passed, we children had grown up and all but one had departed home.

It happened after my mother was summoned to New York to care for her sister who had had a nervous breakdown (precipitated in part by the nightly parade, on TV, of cargo planes bringing home bodybags from Vietnam, including one containing the shattered remains of a young man she had cared for when he was a child). The gold bracelets were going to pay for the plane ticket, but her horticulturist brother helped out and Thaïs, at fifty, left Trinidad for the first time, arriving in New York wearing her gold bracelets. There the land of opportunity allowed her, though still an illegal alien, to work at childcare and household help, care for her sick sister and train as a geriatric nurse. For the first time her gold bracelets were secure. She had the means to eat, pay rent, spend on the education of her, by then, US-relocated grandchildren, buy gifts, send money home to care for her own last child left behind, furnish an apartment and live in a degree of comfort that she had never imagined.

Well-meaning friends warned her of muggings and the risks she was taking in wearing her gold bracelets on subway platforms in Brooklyn. But she persisted and was lucky. (Those were the days when New York City, not Port of Spain, defined dangerous). In her final years, my mother added other bits of gold jewellery but her prized possession remained her twenty-four carat gold cocoa-pod bracelets, that gift from her prescient father.

2

MONTY AND MARILYN

Last night, Sandra watching Oprah, and she making sign for me to come and watch too. I get a beer from the fridge because, you know, I can't watch them women show dry so. Well, I stretch out on the sofa, put my two foot on top of Sandra lap, and I watching too.

You know how Oprah does have guests coming in the studio to talk about different things? Well, last night she had somebody talking about how men and women different. How they are like different species. Well, I see Sandra looking at me sideways and nodding her head at everything this fool on the TV saying. I look at Sandra and say, "You don't believe that stupidness?" She say, "Why not? I see that kind of thing all the time." I say, "Tell me what you does see." She say, "I will say only these two words: Monty and Marilyn." Well, I can't admit to Sandra face that she could be right, but she had a point. Because the story about Monty and Marilyn really make you wonder whether what the psychologist man on Oprah was saying had some truth to it.

My friend Monty was a big, strapping man. He used to go to the gym. He used to jog around the savannah. He used to play football with the boys. And strong? Well, when he shake your hand, you feel like he wringing it off. Well, one day, Monty take in with a belly pain. Everybody say he pull a muscle. Monty try Alka Seltzer, he try aloes, he try *ditay payee* but nothing working. When Marilyn couldn't stand it any more she say, "Is doctor for you."

Well, the doctor look at Monty, he poke this and that, he send him for some tests, then the verdict: Monty have cancer, liver cancer, advanced liver cancer. And nothing to be done. Just so, Monty start to shrivel up. One week, Monty fine, next week,

Monty have belly pain, next week, Monty have liver cancer, next week Monty squeeze up like a orange, and the next week I have to put on suit and tie and go to Monty funeral.

About two months after Monty pass away, phone ring. Is Marilyn. Before I could even say, "How you girl? I was going to call you," she start bawling. "What's up Marilyn?" I ask her. Marilyn say, "Come over now, Leo, I have to talk to somebody. Something has happened."

When I get there, Marilyn eye red, red, but at least she stop the bawling. "What happen, girl?" I ask her. Marilyn pull a phone bill from her handbag. "Monty's cell phone bill," she say. "Look at the date on this one." The date was about when he pass away. Marilyn say, "Look at the numbers." I see that one number come up almost every day, but I don't want to say so; I say, "I see Monty used to make many calls, like his business keep him real busy." She say, "Leo, don't take me for a fool. Why do you think I called you here? You were Monty's best friend and I need some answers." "Answers to what, Marilyn?" I ask her.

Marilyn look at me straight in my eye and say, "I want to know what you know about who he was phoning every day. Look at the bill, Leo. I'm not making this up. Look, it's right here. See that number? Nearly every morning at nine o'clock, he called that number."

I start to feel uncomfortable because I could guess where she heading. "Why you letting a little thing like phone bill bother you? Monty was your loving husband, not so?" I say. "All a we uses to admire how when you go out, Monty always dancing with you and hugging you up. Remember your silver anniversary how he propose to you again, in front all a we at the party? What else you could want to know?"

Marilyn not budging. "Who was he doing business with to call almost every day? On Saturday? On Sunday? Nine o'clock nearly every day. And look," she say, pulling out more bills, "this is one year's bills from his drawer, same number, same time. What's going on?"

"I swear, Marilyn," I say to her, "I know nothing about this. Monty was my best friend, but I don't know nothing about this phone business. And if I don't know, it can't be anything serious.

Look, remember when he had that trouble with the house? And the bank was going to foreclose? Monty come to me first about it, even before he talk to you. Yes, is true. He didn't want to worry you. Remember the incident with his sister son and the police and the drugs? Who you think Monty confide in to get lawyer? Me! So I telling you, Marilyn, you can forget about these phone bills. If I don't know, is not important."

One week later I get a call – Marilyn again. This time, she not bawling, but she sounding determine. "Look, Leo," she say, "come now." So, I jump in the car and I go and in two-twos, I reach. "Leo," she say before I could even sit down, "I found out who it is." She give me one hard stare so I can't even pretend I don't know what she talking about. "I rang up the number and a woman answered the phone. I told her who was speaking and I asked her who she was. She told me her name is Tricia and she could guess why I'm calling her and if it is about Monty. I told her I saw that my husband used to call her every day and if she could tell me why. She said why do you think? I came right out and said you two were having an affair? She said what do you think? I said why else would he want to call you every day? She said you're right. I said I want to meet you to talk about it. She said yes, I could do that. I always wanted to meet you. I said what about Veni Mange for lunch on Friday? She said yes about one o'clock."

★   ★   ★

Men are really something else. You know what Leo told me last night? He told me that his best friend, Monty, you know the one who died a couple months ago? Well, it seems that Marilyn, Monty's wife, told him that Monty was having an affair with a woman for more than a year and she didn't know about it. And you know how she found out? It was the cell phone bills that showed the number coming up often and Marilyn called the number and spoke to the woman. Yes, she spoke to her. And more than that, she took her to lunch – Veni Mange, no less.

When he told me this, I said, "Leo, what do you think about Monty having an affair?" He said, "Look here, Sandra, that is the man business. If Monty did want to have an affair, is he business."

"And you didn't know?" I asked him. "Sandra," he said, "we was best friends but we never discuss wife or outside woman." I said, "Leo, I didn't ask you whose business it is or isn't. I'm asking you: what do you think about Monty having an affair?" He said, "Sandra, you not listening or what? I just tell you, that is the man business, not mine."

I don't know if he was playing stupid to avoid answering the question, so I took another tack. "Leo," I said, "how you find Marilyn handled it?" He said, "All yuh woman is too much trouble. Why she couldn't leave it alone? The man done dead and gone. Why she have to be digging up in he phone bills? Why she have to call the woman? And go and meet her? Why go looking for trouble?" "Looking for trouble," I said, "who had an outside woman when he had a wife? Who was looking for trouble?"

Leo said, "Sandra, all that is so, but Monty did love Marilyn, he didn't leave her, he never ill-treat her. Marilyn had everything she want. You self use to say how nice her house is and how many nice vacations they went on. Why she couldn't leave that alone? Now she gone making trouble for herself." "Leo," I told him, "how you think she feels now, knowing everything was lies and cover-up?" "What lies and cover up?" he said. "He lie? He never lie to Marilyn. Monty behave decent. He never put anything in her face. She choose to bring on her own heartache."

"You don't think," I said to him, "that Marilyn is beating-up on herself now for trusting him? She probably feeling embarrassed remembering that twenty-fifth anniversary party last year, when Monty proposed again – thinking that when he was in bed with her, that maybe he was imagining he was with the other woman."

"What is the problem with that, Sandra?" Leo said. "I know for a fact that Monty did love Marilyn. Look how he provide for her. Marilyn was Monty queen."

★   ★   ★

When Monty's wife called me, I wasn't really surprised. I was kind of expecting it. You can't be a successful "outside woman" without some understanding of the "inside woman". So, when she called, I was very pleasant. She asked whether Monty used to phone me up every day and if I was his mistress. I thought to myself, Monty's dead and gone. He left two women behind. We might as well behave civilised about it. So, I told her, "Yes," and she said she wanted to meet me and would I join her for lunch on Friday? When I got there, I told the maitre d' I was there to meet Mrs. Turner. He pointed to where Monty's wife was sitting. I looked and I saw an attractive woman in her early fifties. She was wearing glasses, looking at the menu. Her hair was cut in that stylish low cut that older women like. She was wearing a black pants and a pretty embroidered Indian-style khurta. Looking at her I felt a little uncomfortable. I wondered what she would make of the tattoo on my ankle. I tried to pull up the neckline of my top and pull down the hem of my denim skirt. I felt I was back in third form and I was waiting outside Sister Bernadette's office. But, as I looked at her again, I saw the head bowed over the menu, the hand twiddling with the thin gold chain around her neck, she looked vulnerable, and I felt a little sorry for her.

I went up to her and introduced myself. "Mrs. Turner, I am Tricia."

She turned her head, stood up, took my hand, nodded and smiled. "Tricia, call me Marilyn. You want to sit over here? It's cool by these crotons. What would you like to drink?"

We sat and she signalled the waiter. "Ronnie, make that two coconut water and put a double gin in one for me please. And we will have today's special."

I couldn't stop myself. "You are younger-looking than I thought you would be."

She glanced down at her hands in her lap, twisting round the thick gold wedding band. "And you are older than I thought." She looked up. "How old are you? Late thirties?"

Well, that is not a question I answer directly. "Somewhere there. I'm no teenager, if that's what you thought."

She sat up, leaning slightly forward. "You know something, Tricia? I never thought I'd be sitting down to lunch with my husband's mistress." She rested her chin on intertwined fingers, elbows on the madras-print tablecloth. "How long you and Monty were together?"

"Not long. Just over a year. We met one night at Trotters where I stopped for an after-work drink with some friends."

She nodded slightly. I felt encouraged to say more. "He was there alone and he came over to my group to talk with someone he knew and we got introduced. We all had a few drinks together and then he dropped me home because my car was at the mechanic."

She closed her eyes at this point and I went on. "The next night he came round by me again. I had forgotten some papers in his car and he came to return them. He came in for a drink and we chatted for a while. Then he started coming round regularly."

The drinks came and I was glad for the distraction. She took a long draught of the gin and coconut water and set the glass down. "So, you didn't have a boyfriend or husband or anything?"

I sipped slowly through the straw. I wasn't sure how much I should tell her. "At the time, I had just separated from my husband and he was giving me a hard time, ringing me up, harassing me. Your husband and I used to talk about that. He used to ring me up and we would talk. But you know that already."

She nodded, leaned back in her chair. "And?"

"And things started getting serious. I had borrowed money to fix up the flat I was renting. Your husband was very kind and helpful. I was glad for the help-out."

The condensation on the outside of her glass had now formed fat drops. She turned her attention to the glass, using her right index finger to trace small circles.

"Did you know that he was a married man?"

"Yes, he was wearing a ring and I asked him. He told me that he was married almost twenty-five years."

She dropped her hands in her lap and looked down at them. I could see her twisting around her wedding ring. "And that didn't bother you?"

I can't abide it when people imply I'm to blame for a man horning his wife.

"Well, I didn't go looking for him. He came of his own free will. I never asked for anything. He gave me what he wanted to."

She looked up, directly at me.

"You never asked about me?"

72

"Yes, I did. He said that was his private life and I shouldn't go there. I respected that."

I was glad when lunch came. We talked about the pumpkin soup and how we prepare it – she roasts the pumpkin first, I just toss it in the pot; the mahi-mahi led to talk about where to get the best and freshest fish; the callalloo prompted discussion on whether one should add salted meat in these health-conscious times; oil-down would have been preferred to coo-coo. We talked about the merits of coconut milk powder for making ice cream and she told me about her years making ice-cream with hand-grated coconut in a hand-turned churn. I told her about my mother baking bread on the Saturdays of my childhood. We didn't mention Monty.

She then ordered gin and coconut water for both of us, then said to me, "You used to cook for Monty?"

I thought, this is a nice lady; she has been through a lot. I will not hurt her any more. I said, "No, he used to say he ate already… at home."

She nodded with a wide, dreamy smile, making her face so much younger, happier. She looked beyond me into the distance. "Monty loved home food. First thing when he came home, he would open the pot and whatever it was, he would smile and say, 'I see you cooked my favourite!' " She looked directly in my eyes and we both laughed at this.

I said, "The way to a man's heart…" and she added, "…is through his stomach." We laughed again. I feel sure we were both thinking of Monty and home-cooked food, but in two different kitchens.

"Does your mother still make her own bread?" she asked.

I told her my mother had died six years before and the tradition died with her. I asked about her ice cream. She said there was no point without Monty to enjoy it.

★   ★   ★

"Sandra," I say, "Monty having an affair didn't interfere with his life with Marilyn." Sandra say, "Leo, you missing the point. If it was Marilyn having an affair and Monty finding out, what you think he would've done?" I laugh, because, in that case, Monty woulda go berserk – beat up both a them. But, I couldn't say that to Sandra, I could only look – she know the answer already. She continue, "And if he found out after Marilyn died, what would he have done to the feller?" I remain speechless, both a we know Monty's temper.

"Yes, Leo," she say, pushing my feet off her lap, "I will tell you what would've never happen. Monty and the hornerman would've never become good friends. You would never have found them liming on weekends with each other's friends. Look at Marilyn and Tricia, making bread and ice cream together, like sisters, nah, like mother and daughter. Men would never have been like that. Not at all!"

Women! They have to rub salt in every wound.

"OK, Sandra," I say, "you win this rounds. Mars one way, Venus the next. But listen well. Don't let me catch you with some other feller or it will be the battle of the planets." The woman look at me hard, reach for the remote and turn off Oprah. "Leo, you feel you could catch me doing anything? I too fast for you!" She laugh, turn away and she gone in the kitchen. I laugh too because I know is only joke she making, not so?

THE TALISMAN

Margaret stood near the edge of the cliff, her gaze wandering over the sea. There was Tara some distance away – she could see her out of the corner of an eye – hurling pebbles at the foaming wave crests. Their argument that morning still rankled. It pained Margaret, this new distance between them, but she was sure she was in the right – after all, her concern was purely for Tara's own good. A deep rumble vibrating through her feet and a tearing sound behind her interrupted her thoughts and she swung her head round to the source. There, on the slope above, a man, cutlass in one hand, crocus bag and stick in the other, locks swirling about his head, was hurtling towards her on a slide of rolling pebbles and loose dirt. She jumped away from immediate danger – the cliff's edge and his likely trajectory. He skidded to an abrupt halt midway between the two women.

He did not look towards either but both women looked at him. Locks screening his face, he leaned towards a fallen coconut, slapped the tip of the cutlass into it, and swung the blade into the crocus bag, freeing the nut with the stick. The blade snicked into another nut that was also despatched into the bag. He then flicked his wrist sharply, sending the cutlass plunging into the ground, where it hummed in quivering, diminishing arcs. He looked directly at Margaret, his legs bridging the path, his bare toes tensed, holding the earth.

"You enjoying the sea?" A trace of a fake Yankee accent.

Margaret nodded.

"Where you from?" Again, that false intonation.

"Diego Martin." She pronounced it *Digger Martin*, with a more colloquial emphasis than usual.

"Oh… you is local people…"

His voice drooped, sounded Trini, sounded disappointed. He rested a foot on the cutlass handle. Tara turned to gaze at the horizon, a thin line of bright steel, where the leaden sea met the iron-grey sky. Margaret could not easily distance herself from his attempt at engagement; he would think her rude, snobbish. Her nod cued him to continue. "The water rough today, like it coming from far, far." Having paid her dues to courtesy, and not wishing to encourage him further, Margaret returned to the rhythm of the crashing waves. She could feel them undercutting the ground on which she stood, slamming into gaps and cracks, dislodging every weak particle, sucking out loose grains, tugging out boulders. He tried again. "But it still nice to look at."

He squatted over another coconut, ran a slow finger along the cracks in its grey surface, and placed it in his sack. He levered himself up, yanked the cutlass from the ground and slid the blade into a leather sheath around his shoulders. Tara was now looking at him with open curiosity and, as he saw this, he moved across, closer to her. So did Margaret.

"You staying here?" he asked

Tara smiled and inclined her head.

"In the guesthouse?" His head gestured to the all-inclusive bar, restaurant, post office, guesthouse.

"No. In a house up the road."

"How long you here for?"

"Couple weeks, maybe."

"So you come for a sea bath?"

"Not really… posting a letter… taking a walk. What you doing here?"

"I just come to collect nuts."

He came towards her, holding out his hand. "Shiloh."

Tara took his hand in hers. She looked into his eyes and then looked, with a start, at a dark stone hanging from a cord around his neck.

Following her glance, he held up the pendant, shaped like a fat water drop, its colour, the deepest black, intensified by a bright white inclusion in its middle and a black dot within that gleaming white. An accident of geology and sea action had made an eye

76

inside a tear drop. It was framed in a mesh of string with a cord of rough plaited fibre. Tara reached out and he let her cradle the pendant in her palm. The back of her hand grazed his chest.

"You make this?"

"Yes, coconut fibre. The stone from over there." His chin indicated the dark cliffs bracketing the bay.

She let the pendant slip from her fingers to fall back against his chest. "Strange… unusual… like it could see."

"That's true… this eye looking out for me." He paused a while, his gaze dropping to his feet. "I from town, like you; but I leave Babylon and confusion." He paused again, looked out to sea for a long moment and then he continued. "I find peace now… with this."

The flat of his palm covered the pendant, pressing it tight against his heart. It was oddly like making a pledge, Margaret thought.

Tara smiled as he continued. "I have a little place where I does grow things." His right arm pointed behind, beyond. "I does bring stuff down here to sell. Best on the north coast." At Tara raising a quizzical eyebrow, he expanded, "My place real nice, peaceful. It even have a river."

As his arm flowed through the air between them, tracing the slow rolling of a river, the plunging sun framed his silhouette against piled red and purple clouds sheening the black teardrop. Tara was now gazing at him, her dark eyes transfixed, as if at an apparition from another world, bringing to Margaret's mind a painting that she had once seen – the enraptured face of Bernadette at Lourdes. She turned away quickly to look at the dimming streak of light soon to be extinguished by the dark sea merging with the sky. She read there a warning of encroaching night, the two of them in darkness, alone with a stranger, "We should go back now."

Shiloh's gaze stayed on Tara's face. Margaret led the way up the slope, her short curly mop of black and grey hair, like a raincloud. He picked up his bag and followed her, Tara behind. He addressed Margaret, "Come and see where I living. Is heaven."

She turned slightly towards him. "I don't know. We'll see."

"Come tomorrow. Come any day."

Margaret didn't answer. He spoke again. "I down here by the shop every afternoon."

They continued climbing in silence. At the top, as the women were making to move off, he made another attempt, "Look, take my number." He called out his cell phone number.

At a bend on the darkling road, they looked back. He was there, straddling his lumpy bag. Before bed, both women entered his number into their phones.

Next morning, they sat on the bench under the half-umbrella shade of the flamboyant, stunted on the seaward side, leafy, lacy on the sheltered landward side. The fragrance of Margaret's mint and camomile tea mingled with that of Tara's freshly brewed Arabica. The two sat in Trappist silence, intent on the silver ocean ahead. Their unresolved argument of the morning before lay heavily on Margaret's stomach like chronic indigestion, one that even the herbal brew could not relieve. She knew that Tara blamed her. On reflection, perhaps Tara was right – it wasn't her business to interfere in Tara's life. She felt she must make amends, break the silence somehow. She chose the last evening's encounter.

"You didn't find that meeting strange yesterday?"

Tara didn't alter the direction of her gaze. "You mean the Rastaman by the sea?"

"Yes. You weren't afraid?"

Tara turned to face her. There was a derisive little smile on her face. "What it had to fraid? Was only a man picking up dry nut."

Margaret bristled. "I don't know what you saw, but I saw a man with a cutlass. We were alone. We had no way of escape."

"But he didn't mean no harm. I find he was quite friendly."

"You are forgetting where we live. Two hundred and fifty murders since January and it's only June."

"Well, the story I hear is, is gangs, is guns, is drugs."

"And they also say that if you take away the murders from domestic violence and take away those from gang warfare, the murder rate is nothing to be alarmed about. But who in their right mind swallowing that?"

In silence they sipped their drinks, while looking at the sea. After a minute or two, Tara picked up the conversation.

"But ent that is why we here? For peace and quiet in the countryside? And too besides, is safer?"

"It's quieter, for sure, but I'm not certain about safer. What about the army raiding marijuana fields in the hills, random attacks, trip guns, guard dogs, shooting..." Margaret's voice trailed off.

"You find he look dangerous?"

"No, not really. If it wasn't for the cutlass, I wouldn't have worried."

Margaret contemplated the tree above, its flame flowers with one white frilled petal. Just that little accent, that tiny flash of white, and the red is shown up as so much more intense. Margaret closed her eyes. Could it be, she wondered, that it is in contrast we see things more vividly, like how you can focus better with closed eyes? As the shade shrank tighter, drawing closer to the tree trunk, Tara stood, moving across in that jerky, awkward way of hers, to take Margaret's mug. "Why you think he invite us by him?"

Margaret looked up. "Perhaps he thinks we're rich and he could befriend us to get money?

"Maybe he just want us to see where he living. Just harmless hospitality. He living here and we only visiting."

"I find it hard to trust so quickly."

"That ent so. You take me in and I was a complete stranger. That was trust."

"You had to trust me, not the other way round."

Tara took the mugs into the kitchen and when she returned, she resumed the conversation. "I feel he harmless. No different from you."

"That has not been your whole experience of people, has it?" In Tara's silence, she continued. "You surrender yourself so easily. People see you as naïve."

"I find you overprotecting me. From since I small I taking care of myself."

"You are still recovering from that... that... episode. You're not better"

"I better. I plenty better. The problem is, you don't want me to be better. I feel you want me to keep on needing you."

"I only want you to get truly well. Able to fend for yourself with confidence."

"You don't get it? I feel stifled, like I'm in intensive care... and you over me all the time... constantly checking my vital signs."

"I want to protect you, even from yourself."

"You rescue me that time from Tino... I can't forget that... I grateful for that... I owe you, but you don't own me."

"You don't owe me anything. I'd do the same for any desperate girl. What I can't understand, now you've brought it up, is why you would want to go back to Tino. He abused you, threw you out on the street and yet you write him a letter to ask if he'll take you back?"

Tara hurried back towards the kitchen, leaving Margaret to grapple with her inner turmoil. The girl was badly scarred in so many ways. She had seen some actual scars, long, slanting, white scars across a brown body, across her upper arms and thighs – putting Margaret in mind of those slashes on the trunk of a rubber tree for draining sap. Did she do that to herself or was it someone else's work? Either way, there were serious issues that needed to be resolved so that Tara could come to a better understanding of herself. Where she had picked up Tara was clue enough about her life; Margaret knew very well what work girls like Tara were doing, dressed that way, alone at night on that infamous street that swiftly turned pretty young girls and boys into used and bedraggled creatures. Had she not, at a time that haunts her still, been there too, looking for Lisa? She couldn't guess what in particular had brought Tara to that state – retching into the gutter, her splayed, red-stilettoed feet damming the wastewater flow – and she did not ask when she took Tara home, bathed her, gave a bed, food, clothes and a chance to heal, to start anew.

In the weeks that they had been together, Tara's spirit seemed to become calmer, but now the girl was restless, craving excitement. She had even written that letter, the one she had posted the day before, the one that had caused the quarrel between them. The letter was addressed to Tino, the man who had thrown Tara out when she refused to perform with a new client something she had found distasteful. Margaret had deduced, from the little Tara revealed, that in the letter Tara asked forgiveness, begged to be taken back. It tormented her that girls like Tara didn't know how to protect themselves. They didn't even seem to believe that they were worth protecting, worth anything.

Tara returned from the kitchen with a packet of Rizlas, the roller and her little carved teak box. She rolled two cigarettes, lit them and handed one over. The rising smoke encircled them in its calming, herbal embrace. She sat, her back against the solidity of the tree trunk, its scrubbed wrinkled folds like the skin of an elephant's leg.

"So, why you think he invite us?"

"The Rastaman? I can't figure out a motive, except as I said before, he thinks he can get something from us." Margaret closed her eyes, to shield them from the smoke.

"We meet him by accident… he invite us just so… I don't think it was plan."

Margaret looked up at the flamboyant again as if to find guidance there. If there was any on offer, she couldn't discern it. She shrugged.

"I get the feeling you think we should go. Why?"

"Me, I just curious… the idea of going to bathe in a pool in a river… and, another thing… nah, don't bother…"

"What is it? Tell me… go on…"

"I know you going to find this stupid…"

"Do I ever call you stupid?"

"OK… OK… is partly curiosity, partly the pool… but the real thing is…"

At this, Tara turned to look directly into Margaret's eyes and continued.

"Is that pendant. The seeing-eye pendant around his neck… you see it too… is like something magic… He say that since he wearing it, it make him calm, make him live good… It make me trust him."

"I suppose that things like that can have an effect on people. My mother wouldn't leave the house if she wasn't wearing her miraculous medal pendant. But, I'm not so sure about nowadays. In the old days, I would have gone without a second thought, no question. You could trust anybody then. Sometimes I don't recognise this place… it's like a foreign country with people I can't figure out… it's become a puzzle… a puzzle that could blow up at any time."

Tara rolled up a sleeve of her T-shirt, picking off an errant ant that had strayed from the tree on to her arm. She set it on the ground, watching as it scrambled determinedly back up the tree.

"I going." Her voice was strong, resolute.

"Why?"

"I tired of this place."

"I can't let you go."

"Let? …Wait nuh, is '*let*' I hearing you saying? I is a free woman, don't forget that… Nobody don't have to let me do nothing." An edge had crept into her voice.

"Please listen. You know nothing about him, where he lives, who he is. It's just reckless, going with a stranger."

"But I did come with you… I was desperate then… I desperate now… Bit by bit I forgetting who I is… Sometimes I don't even know what I want to do for myself."

"And you think you will find yourself by exposing yourself to every danger? First you want to go back to the streets to be sent out to pick up strange men with kinky tastes and bizarre demands… and now – an unknown Rastaman?"

Margaret leaned over and ran a finger along a long stripe, stark white against the brown skin of Tara's exposed upper arm.

"You want to be driven again to… this?"

Tara dropped her head on her clasped knees, convulsed with silent sobbing. Margaret sat beside her, rolled down the sleeve and ran a stroking hand along it. She realised that Tara wanted to prove she could take care of herself, that she was an independent person. Going off with the strange man was an opportunity for her to do so. Margaret knew she didn't have the power to prevent her. She didn't want to go, but she couldn't let Tara go alone. She would hold herself responsible if anything went wrong. She would have to go along too if the girl persisted with her stubborn determination to court danger. At least two would be safer than one alone.

That afternoon, Tara dressed in jeans, T-shirt and sneakers as if for a normal afternoon walk. Margaret threw on her walking clothes too and they set out. As they neared the village they could see him in the distance, standing outside the post office, watching their approach, grinning widely as they came nearer.

"So, you decide to come? You wearing sneakers. Good. Is plenty bush where we going." And, at Margaret's alarmed expression, he added, "Don't worry, we have it under control." He clicked his fingers and a black mongrel, flopped in the shade, pricked up his ears and came to his heels. "We're off."

He led them along the sea-fringed road where bright white light flashed off sea and road, turned inland, crossed a log footbridge spanning a stream, then darted through a colonnade of indistinguishable tree trunks into darkness. Swinging his cutlass in casual flicks, he opened a living tunnel through the mesh of vines linking the trees. Tara was sniffing the air, inhaling the essences of the extravagant fecund life around. She was looking from side to side, exclaiming at each new sighting – the iridescent sapphire flash of a Morpho, the red flare of a pachystachis, the orange flame of heliconia – a rather exaggerated, touristy reaction to these ordinary butterflies and flowers, Margaret thought – and, she felt, playing up somewhat to the man ahead. She herself was grateful for the rare piercings of radiant sky that speckled the trail, shimmering with sap from the newly cut vines and branches – a distraction from the anonymous calls ricocheting above, the invisible rustlings stirring beneath, which, unseen and unknown, made her uneasy.

The trail led upwards and further upwards, was lost in twists and turns, as were Margaret's thoughts. Sure, at that moment it was just one man and two women, but they were in his space, led by him, at his mercy. Margaret wondered what he had in store for them; who was waiting in ambush, who might be waiting at his place? What a fool she was to agree to this reckless scheme. When things went badly as they surely must, people would quite rightly say, "Those women must've been mad or on drugs to go off with a strange Rastaman in the bush. They were looking for what they got." Margaret's imagination balked at exploring the possibilities of "what they got".

As she stumbled along behind them, there came, without warning, a startling summit vista of freed, brilliant sky, and they emerged, blinking in the raw light. Margaret felt herself exhale as unknown forest trees gave way to familiar cultivars: mango, pawpaw, sapodilla, avocado. Yam vines curled over bamboo tepees, butter-yellow pumpkin vine flowers dotted the ground, pale green ochroes stood erect in their nodes, pendulous, purple melongene hung low. "I have other things growing, over there." Shiloh waved a proprietorial arm towards a distant embrace of dark trees.

His house was a hut in a forest clearing – carat palm-leaf roof, plaited split-bamboo walls plastered with daub, a beaten earth floor. Tara claimed the hemp-bag hammock, hung from poles supporting the tin-roof verandah; Margaret sank with relief on a log bench. She watched as Shiloh pulled up cassava, yam; picked ochroes and melongene; flared a dry-twig fire in the belly of the mud oven; dipped rainwater from a barrel under the verandah guttering and set it on the chula to boil the roots. He chopped tomatoes, onions, garlic, thyme, peppers, diced pumpkin, shredded bhaji and added them to a frying pan of aromatic coconut oil. In the glowing embers, roasting melongene and ochroes split open, spilling sweet seeds, succulent flesh.

"Food ready," he called, dishing up on to four enamel plates decorated with red roses and Canada geese. "Here we does eat with hand, no metal in mouth." The two women sat side by side in the hammock; he faced them on a low stool.

"I hope you don't mind Ital. No flesh, no salt."

"What have you put in this? It's amazing." Margaret tried an ochro.

"Mountain magic."

"I never had bhaji that taste so good… even the bhaji that my aji use to make don't taste so nice. " Tara brought a handful to her lips.

"Hungry belly is the best appetiser. Eh, boy?" A black tail wagged.

"You grow everything you eat?" Margaret asked.

"Almost."

"This place soooo nice… it too, too nice." Tara looked around then directly at him. "I feel as if I could live here… is… is… is like being back to early days in the countryside… no noise, no traffic, no neighbours… like how my aji and aja – my grandparents – uses to live…" She laughed. "Would a be perfect, if it wasn't for no internet."

"It have internet in the shop. You could stay here as long as you like and go down to the main road when you want internet."

"Oh!... Oh gosh... I didn't mean it so... I not looking to... sorry... but thanks... it would a be so nice if... if I didn't get back to... to whatever..."

He sat still, looking down at his hands, which hung loosely between his knees. He said nothing for a while, upturning his palms and looking closely at them, as if to read his future there.

"I have to tell you something... Yesterday, when you was in the post office, I was in the shop next door." He went quiet for a while, then, "I hear your voice asking for stamps and I watch you put the letter in the post box."

Margaret felt a chill. So it wasn't a chance meeting, after all. His gaze was still fixed on his hands as he went on.

"When you cross the road and go down to the beach, I wait a little bit then I follow you. I wasn't there to collect no coconuts."

At this, they fell silent. It was no comfort to Margaret to learn that she was right to have been suspicious of the man. He had stalked them and baited them and now they were alone with him, God knows where, and for what purpose.

"Why did you follow us?"

"I did make a mistake. At first I thought you was tourists. And I woulda try to make a little hustle."

How foolish they were to have come, Margaret thought. Here in the forest, they were alone with him, dependent on him, whoever he was, whatever his intentions. If he couldn't "make a hustle" from them, what then did he hope to exact from them?

He looked first at Tara then at Margaret as he continued.

"And then I find out you was from here. But you did still seem like nice people, even if you from here. I was surprise you didn't mind having a normal conversation with a Rastaman."

Neither woman said anything to his comment. He took away their empty plates and walked away towards where he said he grows "other things". Margaret followed him with her eyes. What had he gone for, she wondered, or worse, whom had he gone for? She glanced across at Tara and was surprised to find her sitting on the floor, playing with the dog, talking to it while stroking its stomach, her long, smooth, black hair loose, like a veil screening her face. She seemed to be in her own world, unaware of what was going on. Had she not understood what he said about stalking them, luring them to this place and now disappearing for what nefarious purpose? She wanted to call out to Tara, to tell her they should try to escape, running back the way they had come, quickly, before he returned. It was insane to remain there and be at his mercy. But, she didn't call out. She feared that she would look an old fool, a silly old fool, and she feared that more than any fate she could imagine at the hands of her captor and his putative accomplices. She closed her eyes and waited; dear God, protect your child, she implored silently, I have strayed from the path of good sense… I have shown poor judgement… but dear God look on me with mercy… please…

The slap of bare feet on the beaten earth jolted her out of her communion. There stood Shiloh, holding in both hands a long golden ripe pawpaw. With a flick of his wrists he twisted it into two halves. A silvery sheen reflected off the exposed uncut cell walls as the orange flesh parted. A knife would have wounded the cells, leaked their juices… Black seeds, gleaming like sturgeon roe filled the orange cavity… Margaret's eyes and thoughts concentrated on minutiae to still her whirring mind. He turned each half of the fruit upside down, inserted a finger, dislodged the seeds, shook them into a waiting calabash and broke the half again, passing a rough quarter to each of his guests. Runnels of sticky juice ran down their arms as they worked their way through the sweet, fragrant fruit. Perhaps it was the ordinariness of eating fruit that gave Margaret the courage to pick up the conversation.

"What makes you think people don't want to be friends with people like you? With Rastas?"

"Experience – the best teacher it have. Is like we Rastafarians have our space where we allowed to be seen and heard. Emancipation Day, when we drumming, is OK, otherwise, every time people see a Rasta, they does cross the road. But you didn't and it make me think you is alright people that I could trust."

Margaret did not know what to say. She looked down, flushing red, embarrassed that he considered her trustworthy, she who had mistrusted him all along and still continued to, in spite of his generosity, his courtesy and his confession. She would not be so easily disarmed. In their silence, he continued.

"I specially wanted people like you, nice respectable ladies, to come here to see where I living... to see how I living."

"And you living real good... real Irie," affirmed Tara.

At this, he smiled, a shy, grateful smile. An awkward pause followed; no one knew how to move the conversation along after that. Shiloh clicked his fingers and the dog rose to his feet and came to put his muzzle in Shiloh's outstretched hand.

"Come boy, let's take the ladies to wash their hands."

He led them along a well-worn path through the forest towards the rising sound of rushing water. When they came to a screen of lianas, he pulled aside the trailing vines, and, bowing dramatically announced, "Ladies, look at it, my precious emerald!" Before them was a river pool, wide, shady, rock-strewn, water and sunlight combining to transmute the reflected deep green of the encircling forest into a living gem. On the bank, white lilies raised their cowled heads above the spreading skirts of their heart-shaped leaves. They took off their shoes, walked to the water's edge, and, ankle-deep in the clear flow, splashed clean their hands and arms. Tadpoles like fat commas, roused and curious, butted their black heads against their toes. Shiloh dived right in, inviting with upraised arms.

"Come in. It really nice."

Margaret stood at the edge, unsure of what to do next. Tara did not pause. She peeled off jeans and T-shirt, stripping down to her underwear. "Is no different from a bikini," she said to Margaret as she walked further into the water, clutching her arms to her chest and shivering with the shock of chilly water. As Tara dived in, Shiloh called out to Margaret, "You can't come all the way here and not enjoy the best part."

Margaret waded across to a giant, flat, riverbed stone and scrambled up it. The slanting sun struck hot. She closed her eyes and began to think about herself and how she must seem to other people, to strangers, like Shiloh. She had not always been like this – anxious, suspicious, fearful. Her earlier trust had been slowly eroded by life – by the change in people around her, by her intimate knowledge of the lives of her rescued girls.

From time to time, she looked across at Tara who seemed so happy, in an excited childlike way. She, Shiloh and the dog were playing at throwing and catching fallen fruit, cavorting and splashing with the abandon of familiar playmates. When Tara joined her on the rock, Margaret saw none of the tension of the morning; she saw in loose limbs and fluid movement, a release, a surrender of her whole being that she had never seen before. The scars on her arms and thighs caught the fading sun, those long gilded chevrons worn proudly exposed like hard-earned tribal marks. Shiloh emerged from the green pool, stood upright, and shook his head to set free the captured water, spraying a benediction over them. Walking to where they were reclining, he lifted the necklace with the seeing-eye pendant from around his neck and placed it over Tara's head. "Peace," he said.

The day ended, draining away both tension and pleasure. In silence they and the dog passed through the dark tunnel carved out of the living green. At the main road, Tara stopped walking with Margaret and turned to Shiloh.

"You remember back in your house, you did say I can stay?… and I say no? … Well, I change my mind… you think I can stay for a little while?"

Margaret, startled at this out-of-the-blue request, looked at her in mute admonition. Tara closed her eyes, blocking any appeal Margaret could make. Shiloh took Tara's hand and Margaret knew that there was no way she could stop her now. She turned down their offer of company on the way back and insisted that she would walk alone. On the road, out of the forest, it was still lingering dusk and she wanted the journey to herself, to assess what this sudden departure of Tara's could mean for herself and for Tara. Back at the cottage that night, she called Shiloh's cell phone number. An automated voice answered, "The number you are trying to reach is either switched off or out of the service area." She then called Tara's number. She heard the phone ring in the kitchen and found it on the counter where Tara had left it in her haste to leave that afternoon.

Weeks passed and Margaret stayed on at the rented cottage. On rain-washed afternoons she walked to the village where she asked about Shiloh at the store. They hadn't seen him lately – he does come and go, they said – sometimes you does see him every day, sometimes, is months and you don't see him. When the post office clerk handed her a letter addressed to Tara, she left it there, saying that Tara would collect it herself. The deepening rainy season gloomed the sky, brought silt downriver, churned the ocean, made the sea less inviting, but she would not leave, tormented by a sense of unfinished business.

So far, she had rescued three girls, but the ache of failure over Lisa, the first one, continued to gnaw. Years before, Margaret had witnessed the slow decline of her bosom friend – at first, from depression, then to drugs to ease the hurt of a betrayal in her marriage, finally to the streets to support the drug habit. How many nights had she spent on the streets looking for Lisa, failing to find her most nights, finding her sometimes? She sensed that many times Lisa wanted to be found, wanted the loving care and support Margaret gave. Margaret offered Lisa a home, a chance to recover, to heal, and it worked for almost a year, but even at her most optimistic, Lisa never became the happy person of old. At Carnival, she assured Margaret that she was ready to take care of herself. She had a job offer, a good one as live-in manager at a small hotel catering to budget tourists, and that all would be well. Margaret wasn't fully convinced but nevertheless gave her blessing and Lisa left. The job lasted only until Easter when trade dried up and Lisa disappeared. People who saw her called Margaret to say that Lisa had been spotted hanging out in a Chaguanas bar where rooms were rented upstairs by the hour. Later reports described her as ragged, emaciated, and sick looking, soliciting at traffic lights downtown. Lisa haunted Margaret's nights, she was the wagging skeletal finger at every feast. "Memento Mei, Remember Me." Which tattered heap of unclaimed human scraps did she become? Margaret made frequent, futile pilgrimages to the hospital, the mortuary, but Lisa was never found, no chance at rescue a second time. "Mea culpa, my fault, I didn't try hard enough." Had she tried hard enough with this one, with Tara? How would she ever know? Tara had made her own choice, true; yet she could not stop trying to save Tara from herself. She would stay on in the cottage, just in case Tara came back and needed her.

One night, a storm that had grown in size and strength from

the moment it left the African coast as a curl of moist air, skirted by the seaside village on its way to wreaking havoc further up the archipelago. The spiralling wind lifted the umbrella of the old flamboyant, ripping its roots from the earth, sending it sailing over the edge. The new crater, filled from runnels of rain quickly churned to heavy slurry, yielded to the pull of gravity, and took some of the cliff sliding into the sea below. She lay awake, listening to the roar of thunder, the siren call of wind, screaming of trees, slick sliding and crashing off the rocks. But she was not afraid; it was out of her control, and in the space wedged open by that thought she saw the wisdom of knowing the difference between the things you can change and those you cannot.

The next day dawned calm and clear, innocent of the ravages of the night before. The cottage was still standing; the bench was there, but little else. She sat looking out at the soft blue sky and gently rippling waters and was lulled into a deep reverie. When the sun at zenith seared through her closed eyelids, she sought respite indoors. She stumbled into the darkness of the kitchen, running her hand along the kitchen counter to feel her way. Her fingers came into contact with something that hadn't been there before. As her eyes adjusted, she saw what she had touched. She also saw what wasn't there any more. In the place where Tara's phone had been resting since that afternoon was a small box. She picked it up. It fitted snugly into her curled palm, but had a surprising heft for its small size. On the box, was a single word in Tara's awkward lettering, PEACE. Margaret turned the little box over in her palm, opened it and looked inside. An eye of stone looked back at her. She walked with the box to the bedroom. She opened the box again, lifted out the talisman and passed its rough cord over her head. The eye felt snug and at home between her breasts. Margaret made a deep, long sigh, dragged her suitcase from the cupboard and started to pull open drawers.

IT'S NOT WHERE YOU GO,
IT'S HOW YOU GET THERE

It's my own fault really. Who send me? Early morning still and your girl already full-on into her *mea culpa* ritual. How so? Well, try this for starters: Boyfriend is waiting for her in Belmont; they have to be at UWI by nine for the workshop; it's eight, she's late and Boyfriend, no punctuality slouch himself, is I-rate.

And, where she went wrong? Just the usual sins of omission and commission. Up at six-thirty and, time-starved, first omission – no power-walk; no oats and oat bran – another omission – only weak tea and just a sliver of time to shower, do teeth and dress; and all this hassle because of a commitment – not a commission, she reminds herself – although she increasingly wonders whether what she has going with Boyfriend doesn't qualify for the self-inflicted sins of commission side of that debate.

For instance, last night, hear him:
"Why you going home so early?"
"I want to be in my own space."
"So, you don't like being here?"
"What does that have to do with my wanting to be in my own space?"

So, this morning, ten to seven, your girl throws on standard uniform for going somewhere nice and undressy in daytime, at least that's predictable – fawn pants, white long-sleeved blouse – all-cotton, soft and easy, made in South Africa, gift from youngest babe – brown leather push-toe Rasta sandals, brown-cotton embroidered Indian shoulder sack – where the cellphone gone? Afro-picking to lift hair – Jah, this going to self-rass soon if I don't do something, and with Gros Michel in hand – eight dollars a

91

pound – organically grown in un-chlorinated water, assured the farmer when they met at SunEaters a week before. "I'm also opening up a quarry on the estate – blue limestone." Wait nuh, something environmentally ambivalent here, not so? But she voiced nothing – tact or cowardice? Does that count as omission? She's never quite sure about these moral dilemmas. Now into white Corolla – only two and a half years hers, after being pre-loved somewhere across the globe, Singapore? Japan? Malaysia? JeezU, we Trinis have the same attitude to sexual partners as we have to cars – you're looking nice? Matters not where you been and with whom. It's the detailing that counts: nice body, nice smell, nice upholstery, nice sounds, and nice shiny bling.

She calls out, "Auntie, you know where I'm going." No answer. Should have read the signs. Maybe they said she was the one who didn't know where she was going; but, nah, no time even for Calvin & Hobbes, Modesty Blaise and Brenda Starr – another omission, but not a sin of – and off, up Royal Palm over the speed bumps, waving to Manmohan at the guard booth and on to Victoria Drive. And then – uh-huh, so this is how it does be? – nosing into a stagnant stream of vehicles. Waiting for fifteen minutes to call Boyfriend and leaving a voice mail to say, "Still in Victoria Drive and all's still."

Nothing moving east to join highway; nothing moving north on highway; nothing moving south on highway; lone SUV enters west bound Victoria Drive, the driver's heavily tinted window glides down a few inches and a Holy Name Convent accent penetrates the stagnant air. "The radio just said that a man was hit crossing the road near the walk-over at Cocorite and the police are on the scene."

Boyfriend returns call: "You called at quarter past seven, where are you now?"

"Still on Victoria Drive."

"What's happening?"

"Nothing is moving."

"So you said. What's causing it?"

"I don't know. All I know is, nothing is moving."

Stop talk for an X-and-brake-squeezing exit from Victoria Drive; man in black car does the sloping eye signal to let her through on northbound lane of highway and she does the cheery smiley grateful wave thing back. Two hatted women, one in white, the other in mauve, on a bench outside the Church of the Apostolic Doctrine, have their backs to the highway and lean towards each other in deep discussion. Must be nice to spend whole morning going to church and discussing scripture; can save a heap of bother with real life. The ladies are under a billboard that declares "Get your car tested, it's the law." Your girl flicks her eyes to the out-of-date test sticker on the windscreen – another omission! If she don't fix that soon, is she they go catch.

On the opposite side of the highway is Mary's backyard with its towering traveller's palm and she can count twenty-four leaf blades in the open green fan. A gold African tulip tree tops Mary's ten-foot concrete back wall, a cluster of red sealing-wax palm fronds, a red umbrella-topped calyandra and a handsome pair of cabbage palms rise, while bright purple and orange bougainvillaea extend thorny arms through a coiled razor wire wall-crest. Mary, neighbour, your girl sends a telepathic message: remember the days when the bougainvillaea alone was enough deterrent?

Your girl now reach outside the first gas station. One car getting gas pumped; one, two, three cars, one, two, three, four maxis speed by on the left shoulder, flash through the gas station, chicane via Ridgewood Towers Drive and Starlite Plaza entrance, dash through Starlite, swish past a dazed woman sweeping leaves into a long-handled dustpan and, screeching to a halt by Jassodra's doubles stall, wedge through the full lane to join the highway again. Booming vibrates from a nearby, low-slung, electric-blue car squatting in its pool of blue neon underlighting. Driver's head – cool dude – nodding to beat; her head throbbing with beat. At Starlite Plaza, Boyfriend calls.

"It's quarter to eight, where you reach?"

"I'm outside Starlite."

"Starlite? Is only there you reach?"

"Look here, I'm doing the best I can. You think I want to be here?"

"I'm not blaming you. It's just that we have to get there by nine."

"Listen up. Why not just drink some coffee and read the papers?"

Just like Boyfriend – gotta keep moving, moving – yeah, like the time they were stuck in traffic on the Churchill-Roosevelt Highway going to the airport, he made her take all manner of shortcuts through Aranguez and El Socorro only to see, when they joined back the highway, the big yellow & blue Courts delivery truck that they were right behind earlier, now about fifteen cars ahead. Did he mind? Hell, no! – he's motion-fixated and he got his fix.

"Chaconia Crescent, a new way home" proclaims a Housing Authority sign on a building site for twenty-two apartments. Another sign says "Heavy Equiptments crossing", and has been saying so for two years without shame outside Four Roads Police Station. Some heavy "equiptments" in the shape of two men, neither in uniform, seated with crossed legs on the upper balcony of the blue and white police station, survey the scene below, as impassive as if they on stage playing Trini Canutes contemplating the waves coming ashore at Maracas. No other human being in sight at the station. A passing brown mongrel lifts a casual leg and pisses on the base of a lamppost adorned at eye-level by a trio of tattered election posters for the members of parliament for the area. Your girl mentally applauds. Little pot hong, you just too short – like one of the said MPs – she smiles here – but you getting full marks for effort.

Red light flashes for pedestrians at crossing on Four Roads junction; woman and baby cross, school children cross, bent old man with stick crosses. Nobody need heed traffic; it's like crossing through a car park. An old tyre stands on its side, half hidden in a hole in the pavement, forming a black arch, looking as if it's waiting for something to be scored through it. Scraps of yellow caution tape, two styrofoam boxes and a KFC paper cup, a paper plate and a broken plastic fork are temporarily trapped in the tall grass growing out of pavement cracks. They are working their way to the drain shower by shower. Oh yes, we need all the drain blockage we can get to ensure good quality flooding next wet season. Two-drop-a-rain and river come down is the Diego story.

Out of Morne Coco Road, cars are converging from four lanes on to two. On the right is the second gas station. "Driving in traffic is tough, choosing the right motor oil is easy" trumpets a billboard. Vehicles squeeze out here too, forcing bumper right in front of your bumper so if you only leggo brakes, is bounce. Drivers staring ahead, wraparound designer shades, no eye contact. Absorbed with cellphones. She lets in one, then another, and an inching phalanx of shining armour from the left, creeping in parallel, advances on its stationary foe. Red Digicel billboard on left promises "Talk free all day". Her cellphone rings; it can't be love, she decides – Boyfriend has to be on Digicel.

"You move yet?"

"Not so that anyone would notice."

"So what you going to do?"

"What you think I can do, eh? Give me some options."

"I don't know. It's not me in the traffic jam. It's me waiting for you."

"Well, I'm certainly not enjoying this either; maybe you will just have to carry on waiting."

"Until?"

"Until I get there or until I don't get there, which ever is soonest."

Nothing like a little puzzle to spice up a dialogue destined for drama and discord.

Up ahead she sees the big tree. January 18 and the tree still trailing Christmas lights in classic chalice arrangement. A big star on top where the tree's head was lopped off two years ago so the star could shine out unhindered by leaves. We certainly have our priorities where it matters. Now it's eight a.m., one hour – a whole sixty minutes – since she left home – three hundred yards behind – and your girl's slipped into reflective, self-flagellating "who send me?" mode.

The white Corolla is just alongside a pavement stall where a weather-worn wood table is piled with breadfruit and green mangoes. There's a dirt gap behind the stall. She can see down the gap and she suddenly loses her grip on the here and now. The references are tilted to the vertical, to shade, to deep green and to filtered light. Old milk tins and mossy clay pots with yellow-stemmed palms, spilt paintbox crotons, heart-shaped anthuriums, leaves screening their *in flagrante* flowers, a mango vert tree, a chenette tree, a zaboca tree, a breadfruit tree, and a scaled-down man standing looking up at a pomerac tree. She follows his gaze. She sees the shoes and pants legs of another man up the tree standing at the axils of the branches coming out at right angles to the main trunk. He has a floral shoulder bag reaching down to his hip. It is bulging with lumps. Red, pink and white stripey pomerac hang from the branches close to the trunk. A pale blue house, secreted among sweet lime and aralias in the back, faces on to this slice of Eden. The scene is shielded from the road by the curving embrace of a tall, thick hedge of candle-flower bush.

When she was small, she used to look for and capture the jumping ladybirds that lived on that kind of bush. Brown they were, wings held in a stiff triangle like sails on their backs, with pale yellow mottles, disappointing to her then that they were not the flat-backed red ones with black dots of real ladybirds on book covers. None that she could make out now, on this bush, though; you had to look close at the underside of the leaf to see them, if she remembers correctly. She has passed this spot every day for the past sixteen years and never once spotted this secret space. Dwelling on the lost decades of childhood, looking for ladybirds inter alia, more lost decades driving past forgotten rustic scenes moisten your girl's eyes – while drying out her throat. Phone rings. Boyfriend; who else?

"Look, it's quarter past eight. What you want me to do?"

"Don't provoke me with that kind of question or I might really answer it."

"If you had stayed the night as I suggested, we wouldn't be in this mess now."

"Wait a minute; I was to spend the night by you so as to avoid a traffic jam? That was the reason?"

"Well, I wouldn't be here now and you there."

"Oh ho! So, I'm to sleep over for convenience sake? That's it? What's good for you must be good for me too? Look fuck you."

"That too could have been on the cards."

"I'm in no mood for your puerile attempts at humour… just go to hell."

Your girl puts an end to the exchange by turning off the phone. She can't take on no more jamming right now; nuff stress with this traffic. Chevrons of joining cars come from the left, from Diego Martin Main Road. On the right is Acton Court – eighteen or so townhouse villas. Fifteen feet of sheer, solid, buff-painted concrete topped by gilt spikes protect the gated community. The grass verge outside, a pavement remnant, is neatly trimmed. Flat cropped ivy has been trained to cover the wall and she sees the main shoots, thick as thumbs. A grackle walks by along the grass. His blue-black sheen ripples along his body as he jerks along; his head twitches towards the ivy; luminous yellow irises peer under the ivy's green skirt. His black beak makes sudden stabbing prods at the space where grass and ivy meet. Intent on his own agenda. Birds, bees, men, politicians, all doing their own thing… irregardless… hmm, birds do it, bees do it, even men and pol-it-i-shuns do it… let's do it, let's take on no-bod-y… tum… dee… dum… dee… dum… humming and drumming a finger staccato on the steering wheel… Humdrums, doldrums, doll drums… nice one… Hmmmm… might as well, your girl thinks, turning on the phone and calling Boyfriend. He answers.

"You! I was trying to get you. Check and see how many missed calls on your phone. You turned off the phone? You leave me here stranded and I can't even contact you to find out what going on."

"I must've been in a dead zone."

"How you could be in a dead zone and you say the car not moving? You wasn't in any dead zone before."

"I'm in no mood for the third degree. I've had enough. I don't know when I'll get to Belmont. I don't think I can go anywhere today. As soon as I get out of this… mess, I am going back home."

"Just so? Just so you say you not going and I waiting here for you all morning? I know I shouldn't have relied on you. You change your mind for every little thing. Did you know Chica offered to take me and I turned her down? She is right there in Cascade; I could have been in UWI all now so with her if you didn't have me trapped here waiting for you."

"Listen, friend, don't imagine for a minute that I have trapped you. You are a free agent. Come and go as you please. You know something? Call Chica; see if she still home; go with her. And listen to me, next time you sick and want somebody to run and get doctor and medicine for you, call Chica too. And next time the bank write to say they foreclosing your mortgage, call Chica to break her fixed deposit to fix up your business; and furthermore, next time you… Look, to ass with you!"

"And fuck you."

"That would have to be rape."

"Bitch."

"Thanks."

Your girl punches the switch-off key and flings the phone on the floor behind the passenger seat. She rests her forehead on the steering wheel for a moment and then, at a blaring horn from behind, she sits up and moves the car two inches forward to fill the gap. She looks up, ahead, and there, before her, are the hills of Le Platte. Indistinct in suffused light, the grey-green shrubby karstic limestone plateau, worn into egg-box topography by time, and gouged by a quarry on its flank, nestles in the middle of folded sierras. The barbs of towers and relay stations pierce the head and shoulder of Cumberland Hill to the right. The newly minted sun, shafting in from the south, sends thick blades of light up the mountain side, underlighting the tops of the trees; a billion leaves are transmuted to a pale translucent gold. Shards of light glance off glossy royal palm feathers and slick coconut spears. Yearning bamboos lean towards the valley, trembling against one another in a flirtatious passing breeze. In the shade below, in the foothills, the air is a still, slaty blue – accumulated exhaust fumes trapped under an early morning temperature inversion. Her left brain whispers – yes, true; answers right brain, but still, but still… Her heart slows; she exhales. Sometimes, girl, you have to admit defeat; it's all, all of it, much too much bigger than you.

Four traffic lanes jerk into where one lane should be, and your girl, in the correct lane, is pushed over the road edge around the southbound loop and goes bumping across the dirt and roots of the flamboyant tree that shades the open space alongside the big drain. A Toyota Yaris billboard rises from a squatter yard to her right proclaiming its inspired message: "It's not where you go, it's how you get there". Now there's something for the ladies outside the church to discuss. How does that fit in with the Christian ethic of sacrifices in this life for rewards in the next etc? What about means and ends, eh? Is the statement a subversive, nah, overt pitch for a shallow, consumerist life? And what of the juxtaposition of the picture of a huge expensive car on a massive billboard in the yard of a ketch-arse squatter dwelling? Hard stuff, hard hard stuff; better left alone.

Your girl's attention drifts back to the road conditions. She counts thirty-eight people standing at the road edge in a strung-out cluster at the Petit Valley junction. Their faces are stamped with resignation. Enough people for two big maxis, but she and they know that it would be a miracle if one comes in the next hour with even one free space. Over their heads Toyota Rav4 exhorts, "Just drive your imagination". She remembers laughing when a local wit declared, "You can't do satire in Trinidad. Trinidad is satire". Remembering this can bring only a twisted smile.

Articulated cranes loom ahead, as sharp a yellow as on a child's toy against the blue sky and over the raw grey cement towers of one hundred and twenty apartments under construction. The whole damn country feels like it's somebody's toy to play with as he pleases – everything reduced to Matchbox, Meccano and Lego – but your girl is not in the mood for any more games. The Corolla is now exactly opposite the entrance to her neighbour-hood, but on the southbound arm of the highway at the point where a slip road links the two arms. Red Digicel's billboard boasts its nationwide range overhead – "From Buccoo to Barrackpore" – and your girl adds, "and back to base", as she steers into the sliplane to cross over the northbound highway and complete the circuit to Victoria Gardens. One lane opens a tight gap to let her ooze across, so does the next; at the last minute, the corner of her left eye catches a gold car flying up on the shoulder and she brakes hard to avoid collision. The delinquent driver dismisses her with a "move yuh cunt quick, woman" signal. She retaliates with a brisk "what the fuck you doing there, jackass?" hand. She glides down a deserted Victoria Drive. Manmohan says, "Like you come back. I hear a man get lick down by the walkover in Cocorite." "Is so I hear too," your girl agrees. She drives into her yard. It is nine am. Two whole hours – one hundred and twenty minutes since she left home.

From the car, she collects her bag and the cellphone, turning it on again. She flicks on the kettle switch, seizes the garlic stone, bashes a cardamom pod, two cloves, a star anise and a fat toe of ginger, drops them into her mega mug and fills it up with boiling water. She spots the *Express* on the kitchen counter and picks it up, turning the pages to the daily horoscope. Sagittarius says, "There's no way to please all of the people. This should be liberating…" Amen! she slaps the horoscope column with a hi-five. The cellphone rings; she glances at the number and lets it carry on ringing. She bows her head over the mug of fragrant brew, inhales deeply and strolls with it and the newspaper out to the gallery. She rests the mug on the wide greenheart rail, folds herself into, then stretches out fully within the waiting hammock. She turns her attention to the comics pages. It's time for your girl to check out what Calvin & Hobbes are getting up to today.

ACROSS THE GULF

Dee drove over the bridge, out of the little cul-de-sac where they lived and started to edge into the sporadic stream of traffic on her right. As she did so, she glanced across to her left and spotted the fruit lady hanging up bananas. "Look, dear," she said to her husband, "the fruit lady early today." She angled left instead, slipping the car onto the grass verge, a short distance away from the fruit stall. "I'll be back in a minute, Harold." Her husband didn't say anything. He didn't turn his head in her direction. She got out, shut the door behind her, walked to the stall and exchanged greetings with the fruit lady and chose a pineapple and some bananas. As she opened her handbag to extract her wallet to pay, she felt a hand on her shoulder. She turned to face her husband, who was smiling in that vague sheepish way he had lately adopted. A sharp needle of irritation shot through Dee – she would again have to go through the palaver of making sure he was belted in properly and the door on his side locked securely. Now they were almost certainly going to be late for his appointment.

She got to the car, rested the fruit and handbag on the roof and tried to open the door on the passenger side to let Harold in. It wouldn't open. She walked round to the driver's side. That door, too, was locked, as were all the doors when she tried them. "Give me the keys," she said to Harold. He looked puzzled, held out his hands, empty palms up. She patted his pants pockets, his shirt pocket, but there was nothing hard there. Harold smiled, pushed his hands in his pants pockets and pulled out two beige tongues of fabric that flopped against his grey pants legs. A realisation was dawning in Dee's head; she closed her eyes to help her focus on it and suddenly it took shape. She looked in through the window on the driver's side. There was the bunch of keys swinging from the ignition, the yellow key-ring face smiling idiotically at her. She looked at Harold. He too was smiling, waiting for her to take the lead. She closed her eyes again. She had to work out what to do next. She picked up her handbag. "OK," she said, "I'm going home for the spare set."

She led him back over the bridge to the deepest shade under the big samaan, guiding him to sit on one of its surface buttress roots – knobbly, ridged benches radiating from the massive trunk. "Wait here for me." Without a backward glance she stomped through the white heat, the puddled shadow of her swinging handbag a cruel metronome to the thudding in her head. Now he couldn't be trusted to do a simple little thing like go home for the spare bunch of car keys hanging on the inside of the door of the cups and saucers cupboard where they had hung for the more than half-century of their marriage. Back home, she collected the spare set, locked the front door, and set off again.

When she got back to the tree Harold was nowhere in sight. She put down the things in her hand on the roof of the car, next to the pile of fruit, looked around and called his name. There was no answer. "Harold!" she shouted, louder this time, an edge to her voice. Still no answer. Maybe, maybe he was playing a childish game, playing hide and seek. She walked round the thick girth of the trunk, calling his name. Where had that blasted man gone? When she got back to the car, she saw the fruit lady waving at her.

"He say he going for a walk," she called out.

"Which direction he went?"

"He went down into the river," indicating somewhere behind her stall.

The river was a paved dry riverbed, through which ran a slimy trickle between rain showers. At the first drops of rain, however, water ran off the denuded hills, sending a brown torrent raging up and up the paved banks, sweeping under the bridge and some- times over it. Today at least it was dry. She looked up and down from the bank. There was no sign of Harold. He could have turned left beyond the first curve, and gone home, scrambling up to the back gate behind the house. Maybe that's what he'd done. She threw her handbag down first to free her hands for the descent. It landed on a narrow shoal of coarse beige sand and fell open, scattering its contents. She let herself down, backwards, like on a ladder, pushing the toes of her shoes with the sensible heels into weep holes and worn places on the side walls, scrambling and grabbing handfuls of the tough razor grass that grew in the cracks.

"This is sheer lunacy," she thought, "if I was to fall, no one would know." She shivered at the image and took her next step with uncharacteristic caution. "I can't imagine what possessed that damn man to come down here." She examined her scuffed shoes, the streaks of mud on her dress, her chipped nail polish. "When I get my hands on him, there'll be hell to pay." She picked up her handbag, hastily stuffed in the items that had fallen out and snapped it shut. Looking around, she was all at once aware of how deep the channel was, how cut-off from the world above – she could see or hear nothing of the heavily trafficked road several feet above her head, could not even hear the purr of her own car, its engine still running. She headed upriver towards the back wall of her house, the toc-toc-toc of her footsteps bouncing off the walls, a signal, she felt certain, to any crouching bandit or vagrant, that here was a likely target.

When she got to a position under her back gate, she slung her handbag around her neck and with both hands pulled herself up, grabbing fistfuls of the abundant scraggy vegetation that had secured a foothold in the worn mortar between the crazy-paving of the channel walls. She came up level with the gate, only to find it locked on the inside. Her calling, banging and rattling drove Sandy and Theo into a frenzy of barking and jumping on the other side. She could hear their claws scraping on the metal gate as they tried to jump over, but there was no human response. She retraced her steps down, sliding now, too filthy and angry to care, ran back along the river bed, her breath coming in gasps from the unaccustomed exertion and from a sudden clenching feeling in her throat that she was being risky and foolish to no good end. When she got to where she had first entered, she climbed back up to street level and sat at the edge of the river channel to make an assessment of her situation. That useless search had taken ten to fifteen minutes, and with her having left Harold maybe five to ten minutes before that, she worked out he had been gone around half an hour. He could walk quite far in that time in whatever direction he had chosen. He had lost nothing of his old stamina.

The fruit vendor looked her up and down.

"You didn't find him?"

"No, he must've gone the other way. I'll have to drive around and look."

Dee marched to the car and opened her handbag to get the spare set of keys. She plunged her right hand in, feeling each item in turn, expecting to make contact with the rounded triangle alarm thingy on the key ring. But she didn't. She tipped out the contents of the bag onto the lid of the car trunk and searched through: house keys, pack of tissues, pencil case, wallet, long tangled scrolls of grocery bills, hairpins, Fisherman's Friend original, tube of hand cream, small hairbrush, black embroidered cellphone case, mucky ball of used tissues, everything damp and sandy, but no car keys. She chucked everything back in the handbag and scrambled her fingers through the pockets of her dress, though too shallow to hold anything. She upended the bag once more, separated the contents again, but the car keys hadn't materialised so she flung it all back in.

"Oh dammit," she thought, "the keys must be still on the riverbed where the handbag fell open." She went back to the edge of the river and looked down. She saw no keys on the little sandbank. She had to go down for a closer look. She exhaled to a count of ten, retraced her descent, and got down on her hands and knees to scrape away the top layers of sand. She uncovered bits of broken glass, a grey rag, an empty motor oil bottle, but no car keys. Another ten or so minutes wasted.

Back at the top, she avoided the fruit lady, stormed past her droning car and followed the little street to her home. She showered, changed, poured a neat Talisker, and lay in the hammock to have a drink and a think about what to do.

Harold had disappeared. The first sip of the warm malt was soaked up by her tongue. He had climbed down to the river. The second sip was absorbed into her palate. He hadn't gone up, so he must've gone down. The third got as far as her tonsils. She had no car, at least none she could use; one set of keys was in the ignition of the locked car, the spare set she had herself lost. Tipping back her head, she sent the last mouthful down; it vaporised up the back of her throat, into her sinuses and then to her cerebral cortex where a thought lit up.

She called her bridge partner, Hazel. "We have to go to look for Harold... Yes, he wandered off... yes, again, Yes, yes, I know you warned me about that... No, I can't tell you now... No, I can't go myself... Come now... when you come you'll hear the whole story."

By the time Hazel arrived, thunderclouds had built and the first fat drops hit the windshield of Hazel's Corolla as they passed the humming Focus with its festive fruit bonnet, the Carmen Miranda of the car world.

"How much gas does that car have?" Hazel asked conversationally.

It hadn't occurred to Dee that she should be concerned about gas while Harold was missing, but now that Hazel had brought it up, she had to think about it.

"Too much... Pity I filled up yesterday... It could go for days in park I expect... but the car, the keys, the gas are the least of my concerns right now... Right now, all I want is to find Harold."

She strained forward, peering at the now warped, now blurring images, her eyes darting from one side of the road to the other while Hazel quizzed her about the morning's misadventures.

"I can't picture you climbing down into the river, running up and down looking for Harold. You really went down in the river by yourself?"

"I didn't know what else to do. When the fruit lady said he went down there, it was my first instinct to follow him. To see whether he had headed for home, through the back gate."

"You're something else, girl. It's a good thing she didn't say he climbed up the samaan. You would have had to go up and rescue him, like a stranded cat."

As this mental image formed, Hazel laughed. Dee pursed her lips and cut her eyes at her companion.

"I'm glad somebody thinks it's funny."

"Well, if you don't laugh, you'll have to cry."

"I'm not ready to cry yet."

They followed the road that ran alongside the now roiling river, but saw only a few sodden souls trudging under umbrellas. They swung up past the Hilton and Dee thought of the days when she and Harold used to dance to the tinkle of Ralph Davis on piano, there on the terrace overlooking the savannah, not a care in the world, when the hotel first opened at the dawn of the Independence era. Then, they didn't, couldn't foresee that it would not always be thus, that the future held this – he wandering off and she, her heart squeezing at what could be, searching for him in the rain. After it had washed the streets and flushed the drains, the shower pulled back up into the sky, stopping as quickly as it had started. The sun came out, the black tar road dazzled and the river went down. They drove further, into districts they wouldn't dare venture into on foot, but there was no sign of Harold.

"You want to go to the police station?"

"You know they're not interested unless the person has been missing for twenty-four hours."

"It's now what?"

"Three, four hours. If we go to the police station, we would have to wait until somebody bothers to take a statement in longhand and I really don't feel up to spelling every word and then have them say they have no vehicle to go to look for him and did I check with his friends and furthermore he hasn't been gone twenty-four hours yet."

"Let's get you home, anyway."

"I must carry on looking for him but I can't do that while I have no keys to open the car."

"There's never a car thief around when you need one. Maybe we can try to open it with a wire coat-hanger and if that doesn't work, we can call a locksmith."

"I will work something out when I get home. I can't think straight right now."

Back in her neighbourhood, Dee saw the fruit lady packing up to go.

"Look, your daughter left a note on your windscreen."

It wasn't a note; it was a notice. A strip of cardboard was spread over the windscreen, clamped in place by the wipers. The thick

106

red-marker letters had run, but still legible for the entire world to read was the proclamation, 'DADDY IS BACK HOME'.

Indeed, Harold was at home, warm and dry and safe, lying on the sofa, watching cricket on the TV. He paid no attention to her bustling arrival. Dee took the remote and turned off the set.

"Where were you? I have been out of my mind looking everywhere for you."

"Nowhere. I was here, watching the cricket."

"The last time I saw you, you were waiting under the samaan. That was since midday. I went home for the spare set of car keys. When I came back you were gone. The fruit lady said you went in the river."

"I wasn't in the river. A nice girl took me for a drive in a car."

"What girl? You mean Natalie? It was Natalie who brought you home. Natalie is your daughter."

"My daughter? I have a daughter? Imagine that, I have a daughter. Why didn't you tell me that before?"

Dee turned the cricket back on. She went to the Talisker. She needed a drink and a think – a big one of the former, maybe just a little of the latter. Fortified, she picked the phone and called Natalie's cellphone. Natalie spluttered like a pressure cooker with a dhal-clogged vent.

"Why on earth did you let him out of your sight? You know he can't manage on his own."

"How did you find him?"

"A complete stranger called my cell. I was in the gym, doing abs reps with my trainer. I have to get back in shape after Joshua. You realise Carnival is just two months away."

"Yes, yes, yes. How did this complete stranger get your number?"

"He found Daddy climbing out of the river, soaking wet, looking confused. He asked him his name and he couldn't answer. He asked him for a phone number and he mumbled mine."

"He remembered yours. He didn't remember mine?"

"Speaking of which, Mummy, why didn't you answer your phone? I called, must be a hundred times, and all I got was voicemail. On my way to take Daddy home, the fruit lady called out that you had gone with a friend to look for him, so I borrowed cardboard and a marker from her to leave that note for you to see when you passed back."

"I wonder why you couldn't get me on my cellphone... Let me check."

Dee pulled out the phone from its little embroidered case and looked at its blank face.

"Oh my gosh, Natalie. I am so sorry. I turned it off at church yesterday morning. It must have been off since then. Oh gosh, I'm so sorry. I'm really forgetful. Daddy and I are both getting forgetful these days."

"Mummy, you are forgetful... Daddy has already forgotten. When I took him home, he didn't know where his clean clothes were. I had to look through the chests of drawers to find something. At least he is still able to shower and dry himself."

"Sometimes I wonder whether he's deliberately acting up just to annoy me, then sometimes I think he's losing it."

"Daddy isn't acting up. He isn't losing it. He's already lost it. And then, to make matters worse, you go losing him too. Don't let him out of your sight again. Next time he leaves the house, make sure your phone number is on a piece of paper in his pocket. Better yet, print a T-shirt, no, print a few T-shirts with – *My name is Harold. Call my wife if you find me* – and put your cell number below. He should be wearing one every time he leaves the house. In fact, put one on the minute he wakes up in case he wanders off when you're busy. And, keep your phone charged and switched on, even in church."

"Natalie, you have no idea how hard it is to manage Daddy now that he's getting in this state. Some days he's OK, other days, you have to do everything for him. It's hard."

" Mummy, don't you think it's about time you took him to one of those geriatric specialists? His condition can only get worse. The least you can do is get some professional help. Maybe they can slow it down. There are always new drugs and therapies."

It was not the answer Dee was hoping for. She didn't need telling about doctors and drugs. She needed someone to offer to come by and help, to chat with Harold, to take him out. As she hung up, a line from The Mighty Shadow's calypso came to mind, "Old age has no remedy". Yes, doctor or no doctor, there was no cure for getting old. Young people never thought they too would one day be old. If they were lucky. So many friends had been unlucky, losing husbands, cut off in their prime. But then, who were the lucky ones, eh? She picked herself up and went to the kitchen to make an early supper.

What to cook? Food had become both medicine and cult. To the old timeworn simplicities – carrots good for eyes, oranges to ward off colds, fish for brain activity – had been added a raft of foodisms: cauliflower, broccoli, and cabbage as cancer fighters; oats and oat bran to lower cholesterol; raw vegetable juices for the enzymes. It seemed like only yesterday that they were hosting wonderful Sunday brunches – saltfish buljol with coconut bake, Spanish omelettes as big as pizzas, pigs' feet soused in a lip-puckering broth of cucumbers, garlic, onions, herbs, pepper and vinegar, washed down with Harold's wicked rum punch. These days they hardly ate meat, cheese or eggs. Her kitchen was purged of all the baddies – no pastries in which artery-clogging trans-fats lurked, no diabetes-causing sugar and no carcinogenic artificial sweeteners. Gone was almost every joy, she reflected. She kept her whisky hidden – no need to invite censure from her children who, suddenly smarter than their parents, would lecture on what was good, what was bad, for their health. So they were taking ginko, saw palmetto and red rice yeast, had gone as organic as availability and budget allowed. And to what end, eh? She was on statins; he was on Planet Harold.

She steamed ochroes from the backyard, chopped raw poi spinach, grated raw pumpkin and toasted two slices of preservative-free spelt bread. They would have a light balsamic and olive oil vinaigrette emulsified with whole grain Dijon for the bread and vegetables to mop up. And, why the hell not push the boat out to celebrate their having narrowly averted disaster? They'd have a hefty chunk of organic feta, the best in the world, from that Tobago goat farm. The thought of Tobago brought a memory of long weekends spent on the little yacht they had splurged on, trips over to the sister island, on-board parties with other sailing friends, little Natalie and Drew safely asleep in the bunks below. Drew had taken over the yacht now, up and down the islands, the same Drew, she recollected ruefully, who was afraid of the water as a child. Harold had been the good father, so patient with their phobias. Drew had grown to embrace the sea and Natalie had been rescued from the wave of adolescent anorexia that had put two of her friends into intensive care. Did they not remember those days too? Do memories of what parents do for their children reside only in the dimming landscape of the parents' minds? What little treat could she find for his dessert? Ah, he would love some of that fresh pineapple she had got that morning. Oh, dammit, he couldn't after all; the pineapple was still sitting with the bananas on the car roof. And, oh yes, she must put on the kettle for camomile tea.

They watched the cricket, eating their supper under its blue flicker and the drone of the commentator's voice. When the game was over, Harold found her in the kitchen washing up. He put an arm around her waist.

"Sweetheart, let's go out somewhere. It isn't good to be cooped up indoors day after day like this. We could do with some fresh air."

She rested her head on his shoulder.

"OK. We will walk down to the car and pick up the fruit. You can tell me how the match ended on the way there."

"What match?"

"The cricket match. The one you were watching."

He looked at her, frowning with puzzlement.

"What's got into you? I've been reading all afternoon."

She held his hand as they walked down the long-shadowed street. He carried a basket for the fruit. The warmth of the engine had dried the car and wrinkled the windscreen billboard. Dee remembered she hadn't contacted the locksmith yet; he might not come out so late. She stretched over the car roof and picked up the pineapple. As she did so, something slid off the roof and clinked on the tarmac. Harold bent down, retrieved the object and straightened. For just a moment, Dee caught a flicker of an old, familiar Harold in the delight and recognition in his face and voice.

"Look, I've found the keys."

Dee rested the pineapple back on the roof, took the keys from his grasp and unlocked the door on the driver's side. All the door buttons sprang up. Dee put the spare keys in her pants pocket, piled the pineapple and bananas in the basket, put the basket on the back seat, folded the message board and chucked it in the back too. She opened the passenger door for Harold, saw him belted in, shut the door, walked back round to the driver's side and got in.

She wanted to drive and drive and drive. Back into time, back to when Harold could talk to her, read her mind even. It was so lonely, being with him, yet alone. There was so little held in common to draw on, to reminisce on, together. She felt unmoored, adrift. So, is this how it goes, while you're coasting along, not paying any attention, you're slowly sliding into irrelevance and pretty soon you become an irritant, a nuisance, then a burden? She saw herself and Harold heading there, along that road, at different speeds, yes, but towards the same chequered flag. She glanced over at him. His looks hadn't changed much, still handsome with his curly greying... Oh, damn, she hadn't called the barber to explain why they hadn't kept Harold's haircut appointment that morning. She exhaled deeply, suddenly too weary. Harold looked across and touched her knee. With that gesture, his eyes for a moment lost the vacancy that had become resident there, and he gave her a smile in which she read things about the two of them that words couldn't say.

She drove towards the sea. They sat out at the little bar and watched the yachts rise and fall at their moorings. Dee matched the rhythm of her breathing with their movement. She and Harold held hands. The waiter came. Harold sat up with his still sprightly athletic posture, took charge and ordered, "Two Bombay Sapphires with coconut water and a curl of lime rind. Put lots of ice." He squeezed her hand, saying, "Your favourite drink." She gave him a little smile and closed her eyes. When the drinks came, they toasted long life, good health and happiness – gifts they had already been given in abundance and had almost used up. The sinking sun cast haloes of pure light around the residual rags of rain clouds. Wide streamers of gold shivered on the heaving and sighing waters, across the gulf from where they were to where they couldn't see. They held hands while the purple night deepened, its heavy velvety chill descending, cloaking their shoulders.

GHOST STORY

Any day of the week, Sunday to Sunday, you seeing Ghost walking up and down the narrow road that winding through our little valley. People in car swishing by weaving round him, careful not to bounce him, because he walking in the middle of the road. Ghost wearing boots, like discarded army boots, black heavy, lace-up boots, and where you expect to see socks, you see very dark brown, stringy, hairy calves leading up to ropy thighs with the wide legs of khaki shorts flapping around. Holding up the shorts is a wide, black leather belt – more army throw-out stock. And that's it for clothes. Ghost always bare back, back running with sweat, and he have a full, lumpy crocus bag fling over one shoulder or across the whole two shoulder. In one hand he holding some kind a tool: a three-canal cutlass or a hoe or a grass-swiper; sometimes is only a long stick with a hook at the end.

We used to wonder how come police don't ever stop Ghost to ask why he breaking the law, walking around the place with bare sharp tools when honest gardeners wrap up their cutlass and thing in gazette paper to keep within the law. But is when you look at Ghost face you know why nobody don't stop him to ask no question, because Ghost face always set-up, vex-vex, like he about to cuss you, his eyes cokey – one eye looking so, next eye looking next way, and Ghost have a wild look, the raggedy beard and the thick-thick locks, hanging in two-three dense clotted mat like a old coconut fibre doormat. You feel anybody could put God out their thoughts to even say morning or evening when they pass him? Too besides, he striding up and down purposefully like he have somewhere to go and he can't be late, and you fraid to get in his way. But most of all is because he looking don't-care, and don't-care is like untouchable to us ordinary people.

112

But that don't mean people didn't talk to Ghost at all. We used to have plenty conversation with Ghost, after all, is only good manners to exchange a few words with a person who spending more time in your yard than you. Everyone in our cluster of little houses scrambling along the face of the steep hill-slope have a favourite Ghost story. When we meet up at one another house for breakfast after church on a Sunday morning, was always a chorus of complaints about Ghost. Marjorie say one time she hearing the dogs barking and she gone outside to check. The dogs and them running around and around a orange tree and she look up and see Ghost. She say, What you doing there? He say, I picking some orange. She say, Get down, get down at once, and he get down. She tell him, When you want something, you must ask for it. And she tell him to get out her yard. Next morning, she hear someone calling, Morning ma'am, morning ma'am, at the gate. Marjorie in the middle of preparing breakfast buljol, but she go outside. Is Ghost. I come for some orange, he say. She say, OK, and she lead him to one of the tree. Pick from this one, she instruct. Ghost shake his locks. Not that one, he say. Them orange too sour. I taking from that one over there. Them sweeter. He pick and pick and when he done he tell Marjorie, Look I pick some for you too, and he leave about a dozen or so in the mop bucket by the back step.

Hazel say she ketch Ghost in the zaboca tree and tell him to come down immediately. He say, I can't come down yet, I have a order to fill. Hazel tell us she understand, because that same afternoon she see the same zaboca self, now label avocados, at the nation's favourite grocery, for ten dollars each. When Nicky tell Sue that Ghost pick out all the nice yellow-flesh breadfruit and he tell her when she see him leaving the yard with the crocus bag bulging, that he leave three more for her and they will be full enough to pick next week, Sue say, But he is a nice man, last week he sell me some really nice julie mangoes, five for ten dollars. Mavis say, He thief those mangoes from off my tree. Sue say, Your julie is the best I eat this season. So it look like he harvest from the one and sell to the other, keeping the fruit circulating and making up deficiencies where he seeing them, like supply-side economics, with him as middle man.

Louisa say, Is people like Ghost who keeping the neighbourhood safe because he always on the lookout, he know everybody times of day and comings and goings and if a strange bandit come in to do real harm, he will see them. She say, We don't recognise that Ghost is our protection. Marlene laugh and say, We should call him Holy Ghost then. But Louisa quickly remind her blasphemy is a sin. OK, sorry, Marlene agree, is like having a kind of informal security and we paying with surplus fruit. Is not surplus, Denise say, is years I watching my young zaboca tree. First year it bear, is only one zaboca, but it big and nice, smooth texture, dryish. Next year three fruit and I waiting for them to be really full before picking and one morning I look for them and they gone. That wasn't no surplus. He coulda pick one to sample for future reference and leave two for my family until the tree start to bear more. Is hard to have a tree in your own yard and have to buy zaboca in the grocery. People sympathise, Yes, we agree, Ghost does be real indiscriminate sometimes.

But Ghost know everybody business and Maureen say he and her husband does talk good and make joke and only last week her husband pass Ghost sitting on the bridge, and her husband ask him when he think the zabocas will be ready and Ghost tell him, Boss them zaboca have another three weeks still, and how Ghost really have a good heart because when her husband was sick Ghost look in the bedroom window and say, Boss I hear you ent too well, look after yourself eh? I go be real quiet. I ent go disturb you. Look I going to shut your dogs in their kennel so they go stop the barking while I here. And then he proceed to pick off all the full limes. When Ghost leaving he see Debra coming in the gate. She hustling, hustling because she had to drop the child by the child father mother as her own mother had to go out. Debra already late for work and she have to hurry up to start preparing lunch, but he stopping her and telling her to bring out a bowl for him. She steupsing but she still bring it out for him. You know what he do? He put down the crocus bag and he drop a couple dozen or so limes in the bowl and he say, Make some juice for the boss, I don't find he looking too good, nuh.

Ghost and we woulda continue like that if the mealy bug hadn't arrive in a schooner-load of plantain and dasheen from

Grenada. In a few months many of the fruit trees off which Ghost was making a living was infested and bearing less and less fruit; in a year, pickings was meagre. Ghost begin to use his intelligence of the area to supplement his income in a different way. Children bicycle left in the yard begin to disappear; Maureen wake up one morning to find the toolshed ransack and lawn mower missing; Denise hear what she thought was rain in the night then next day see pieces of pvc piping lying around spouting water and her six-hundred-gallon Rotoplastic water tank gone. Is now a different relationship start to develop between us people and Ghost. What we use to tolerate before as a kind of sharing was now thiefing. If tree bear plenty, you can spare some – it cost nothing, next year it will bear again; but if you pay good money for something and it gone, you have to pay more good money to buy it back.

People start to lock gate, put up chain-link fence where they was depending on steep drop to be deterrent – some even put in automatic gate – and a barrier came between Ghost and his host. He start to walk the street doing house-to-house visit, calling at the front gate, asking for work. He offering to do garden and clean yard, wash car and so on. Some people feel sorry and take him on but when you make arrangement for him to come Wednesday and you wait and wait for him and he don't come, you bound to get vex, and when he turn up Friday and say he had something else to do, you tell him don't bother you will cut the grass yourself, or wash the car or whatever. It looking like Ghost life always too free for him to get tie down with day and time.

One Saturday morning, Denise pick up the papers from where the delivery man throw it in the yard and she see that a man in the next valley shoot a bandit who he see walking out his yard with his bush-whacker over his shoulder. The papers say the bandit was wounded in the back and was warded under observation in hospital. They print the bandit name: Alfred Thomas. Nobody didn't take it on, nobody think they know any Alfred Thomas, but when Debra come to work that morning she well excited. She calling from by the gate self, Miss Maureen, Miss Maureen, guess what? I hear Ghost get shoot. People was talking about it in the maxi coming up. Before you know it, is all of we people calling round to one another and saying how the Alfred Thomas in the papers is Ghost, and Sunday morning all of us by Maureen for breakfast and the subject is Ghost and the shooting and Maureen ask what we going to do about it.

Marlene say, What you mean what *we* going to do about it? What that thiefing rascal getting shoot have to do with us? Denise, still vex about the water tank and the zaboca, say, It damn good for him, now he will have to keep his blasted tail quiet. Hazel say, That is not a nice sentiment to express on a Sunday morning after coming from church. Denise say, If you did have something thief you woulda be damn vex too. Nicky say, Oh no, what am I going to do now? And she say that she was expecting Ghost to come Monday to clean the yard, the drains slimy with moss, and now she would have to do it by herself and her back not feeling so good these days. Marjorie say that it is a good thing she wasn't depending on him for any yard work, and anyway, yes, she have to agree with Denise that Ghost get what he looking for long, long time. Mavis say, Poor feller, he don't deserve to get shoot for a bush-whacker when, right in the heart of government self, every manjack hand digging deep in the national cash register, and you don't see any citizen rushing out to do a citizen arrest or shoot any of them big thief. Sue say, is people like you self that walk quite to the polling station and stain your finger for them. Is the people like you self put them in power; like all you people don't remember the track record they had build-up when they was in government last time. For the people in this carnival-mentality country everything is a nine-days' wonder. Mavis answer that the last lot wasn't no good either and like we head hard and can't learn no lesson from experience. Sue say Mavis confusing the issue; who is big thief and feathering they own nest, giving big contract and directorship to friend and family is besides the point. Louisa say, ladies, ladies, stop that please; don't bring no politics talk here today. The subject we discussing is Ghost who lying wounded in a bed in the public hospital and at least we could feel good that is not us who responsible for putting him where he is. She say, I asking all of you, who looking after Ghost interest now he get shoot? Ghost is somebody we know and he is a human being too and I personally don't see how we can let him just lie down there in the hospital, shoot-up, and nobody caring if he living or dead. Well, with that second sermon of the day, we focus and we talk and talk and we agree somebody had to go on a mission of mercy and visit the hospital to check-up on Ghost.

Debra serving out some guava juice at this point in the talk, and she volunteer to help out and go and see Ghost in hospital. She say she know about the public hospital, where the different wards is – male medical, male surgical and so on. She say she know the rules and regulations about visiting time and number of visitors allowed and she say how we kinda people wouldn't know how to deal-up with them security who like to rough-up people who wearing church hat and talking and behaving hoity-toity. Denise want to take on the hoity-toity challenge Debra throw down just so, but Louisa jump in quick and say, well, thank you Debra, that's very kind, we appreciate your offer. Everybody agree that Debra is the most suitable person of all of us to tackle the petty bureaucracy of government-run space.

That same afternoon self, Debra set out with a bag of mango, orange and sapodilla we gather up hurry-hurry, to visit Ghost and take him our get-well-soon message. When she come back Monday morning she say, Ghost not doing too good nah: the bullet still inside and he have to have operation. Well, things start to get technical now and is like we have to intervene beyond mango and sapodilla. We send back Debra next day. She don't mind going because she get getting off work early and too-besides, her role now enhance beyond cooking and cleaning – she is the designated intermediary. Her mission is to find out who is the doctor on the ward, when the operation is, whether police pressing charges and so on.

Debra come back and say the operation is for next week Thursday – if the theatre have current and if they get through the backlog from last Thursday when current gone whole day. She say she know the fellow who does make up the list for the surgeon and he say he could put Ghost name high up on the list if he get some encouragement for him and for the surgeon too. All-a-we vex like hell about this grease-palm business. What the hell the oil and gas royalties is for, what taxes is for, what else health sur-charge is for if not to make everything in public hospital and public clinic available for everybody in the public, irregardless, and ent these people getting pay already from we same tax etc. But, after all said and done, all-a-we know is vent we only venting; we know this is not a whistle to blow so easy, when people out there in the know have it to say that even the Head of the District Hospital Authority been seen to be redirecting brand-new hospital equipment and supplies the Health Ministry pay good money for, to his own private clinic. We not powerful but we not stupid; we know the cards stack in their favour not our own and if we play mad and say we going public about corrupt practice, before you could say bribery and corruption, Ghost would be discharge immediately with the bullet still inside him and then what we will do? Paying the same surgeon to do the operation in his private clinic was out of the question. So we agree to shut up, sub up and help out; it will be cheaper in the long run. Eventually, talk done and everybody boil down and agree and pull out wallet and purse. Cash only, no cheque.

Debra continue to visit in the hospital; Ghost get the operation, Ghost discharge, Ghost home recuperating. And Debra bringing us the latest news about how Ghost progressing. That he living up a steep hill over by so, with a dirt track to the house Ghost and his father scramble to build together. And that now that his father dead, is his mother and sister living there with the sister three children. That the sister does do a little hairdressing – braiding, weaving, straightening – and how she expand to nails too with her biggest girlchild helping out, learning the same beautician business because it does pay good, because everybody want to look nice, and that the school the same girlchild pass exam for is only a waste-a-time place; the teachers don't come to class and the children only having sex in the classroom and taking videos with their cellphone and sending it all around the place, and some even selling it on the internet, and how she don't want her daughter mixing-up in that kind a thing, is best she help out with the business and learn something she could make a living with. Debra say to us, all you don't have to study Ghost at all, nah, he mother and sister helping he out. We self wondering among ourself, but of course not out loud in front of Debra, how come poor people does have enough money for hairdos and fancy nails but only buying Crix biscuits and Chubby sweetdrink for their children when the day come, and how come little, little school-children can have cellphone with camera in it and not have books for school, but, in the end, we breathing easy, we well glad that it looking like Ghost pulling through all right. So we listen to Debra and we lay Ghost to rest for the time being as we have plenty other thing to deal-up with.

Outside in the yard, we seeing that the mealy bug finally ecologically controlled by a fast-multiplying ladybird colony they bring in from foreign, and fruit trees flowering good again. Mangoes ripening and falling in the yard – and rottening; zabocas too high in the tree for we older folks to pick – is only iguana and manicou enjoying the fruit. And whole week-a-day, we people raking up and sweeping up and piling up whole heap a rotten mango and carcass of hollowed-out zaboca skin and seed that drop when the iguana and parrot done with them, and we wondering how after one-time-is-two-time and how you never appreciate what you have until it done. Nowadays gardener and them don't want to climb no tree for you. They only coming in a team, cutting lawn zrrr, zrrr, zrrr with the whacker, blowing grass cuttings vroom, vroom and then gone, quick, quick to the next yard, and you standing there like a fool with your purse empty, and nothing you really want do, getting done.

One Sunday morning Maureen hear a voice calling, Morning! Morning! at the gate and she look out the kitchen window. She see a man holding a clipboard. Maureen, wondering what he could be inspecting, go to the gate. On the clipboard she see a checker-line copybook clip to it and a list of names and numbers. He say, Good morning madam, I come to offer my services as a estate maintenance professional.

Maureen tell us afterwards she feel something was familiar but she couldn't say exactly what until the man say, Miss Edwards you don't remember me? Alfred Thomas. She say the name sounding familiar but where she know him from? The man say, I used to get lime and zaboca from your yard. She say she look at him good, good. And in the eyes and the eyes alone, she recognise Ghost. His hair cut flat down to his scalp, his face clean, clean; she say is the first time she see he have forehead, ears, cheeks, chin like everybody else; is only the eyes looking two different ways same time. She say she didn't say the name Ghost out loud because it might have sound too friendly, so she just say, Oh yes, is you Alfred, I didn't recognise you. He say, I seen The Light, Miss Edwards. I was in hospital and a pastor come and show me how I was on the wrong path. He point me in the right direction and now I am save. Miss Edwards, I want you to know you can put your yard in my hands. I am making a exclusive list of client who I select on pass experience. Maureen say she didn't know what to say. So she say, What you will do? Ghost, now known as Alfred Thomas, say he will like to come in the yard and make a assessment of what it will entail. Well Maureen and Alfred Thomas go in the yard and he say he will pick the mango and clean up under the tree and he will do that on Tuesday coming. He write down, Tuesday, next to Maureen house number on the list and he say, Thank you, ma'am and he gone up the hill by where Denise and Mavis living.

So said, so done: Tuesday morning bright and early Alfred at the gate. Alfred tell Debra he come to help pick the mango and she let him in. Well, he pick and pick and full up a whole crocus bag. He tell Maureen the day work come to two hundred dollars. Maureen pay him, then she and Debra had was to go and share mango through the whole neighbourhood, because how much mango one person could eat, eh? Is a setta work to pulp and juice and freeze and who have freezer big enough to pack-up with a setta mango pulp? You tell me. Hazel pay him two hundred dollars the following week to pick out her zabocas and he buy back most of what he pick for a hundred dollars and take the bag with him. He say he have an order to supply the little street-side vegetable stalls. And so it went with the pootegal, the orange, the sapodilla the pommecythre and the grapefruit. Marlene say, Look how we find ourselves paying Alfred to do what Ghost use to do for free. Denise say is a real shame that now the nice big trees bearing in abundance, they become a expense to upkeep and a botheration, if they not upkeep. Mavis say, is like damned if you do, damned if you don't. Maureen say her husband say after one time is two time and he not prepared at this stage in life to break his neck climbing tree for no zaboca and is either they move to a townhouse with no yard or find some other solution.

One day, Alfred come to Maureen yard and he find a big truck park-up in the yard. It mark Green Fingers Tree Removal Service. He hearing brrz, brzzz, brrrzzzz. When he look, he see two big man with a chain saw cutting down the pomerac tree, branch by branch from the bottom branch. He rush for the man holding the saw and start to pelt cuff. The man drop the saw and it start to race around by itself in circles till the next man catch it and turn it off. What you think you doing? Alfred challenge the man. The man say, the lady here call us to cut down the trees. Maureen hearing the saw stop and hearing the commotion come out to investigate. She see Alfred on the ground between all the leaf and branch and the red star-spatter of buss-up pomerac bawling like a little child who get plenty licks. Miss Maureen, Miss Maureen, how you could do me a thing like this? Is how long I know all you? She say, Alfred, stop thinking you could take me for a fool. I done with paying you hundreds of dollars for picking my fruit from my tree what I plant in my yard and then you buying from me for next to nothing. Maureen turn and start walking back to the kitchen. Alfred roll on to his knees and start crawling behind her calling, Miss Maureen, Miss Maureen, listen, nah. Why we can't talk like two big people? Maureen look back and signal the Green Fingers men to take a five minutes rest.

She never tell nobody what transpire that day with her and Alfred and Green Fingers, but after that, Louisa finding two hand of green fig by the back step and when she check, the big bunch that was hanging down on the tree down the slope gone; Maureen could count on the mop bucket having a few lime or pootegal and orange when they in season even when her tree bare; morning after morning Nicky greeting one or two nearly ripe zaboca on the kitchen window sill and no rotten ones on the ground, and Mavis enjoying not only julie but starch and graham mango with no flies and rotten fruit under her julie tree. The church ladies still regularly meet for tea and sometimes a remark would pass – where you hiding the pommecythre tree, girl – when homemade pommecythre jam on the menu, and a mango sorbet can put in an appearance at the home of someone who can't boast of a single mango tree, and the ladies would exchange knowing winks because, who knows, maybe a Ghost pass in the night.

3

ERASURES

I could not look my mother in the face and ask the question aloud, the one I had avoided asking all my life. The fingernails of my left hand dug into its palm, forcing resolve, as I picked up the writing slate at Mammy's side and wrote, printing each letter with deliberate slowness, "I am fifty years old." My handwriting wobbled. I knew I was going to a place of no return. "It's time you tell me who my real father is."

Mammy was breathing through a sighing plastic tube in her throat. Her larynx was gone, collateral damage in the war against thyroid cancer. I passed the slate to her. She glanced at the slate, then went rigid, staring, as if an expected doodled pleasantry had morphed into a tarantula. As I looked at her face, I felt remorse that I had done this to her, the one who loved me more unreservedly than anyone else in the world. For many years afterwards I tormented myself with guilt about whether I had been cruel, doing this to someone whom I loved and who was very likely going to die soon. But at the time, all I could think was that, if I had handed her a tarantula, it was one that had scuttled its dark, hairy legs in my chest for most of my life; one that I had swallowed back down over and over whenever it had tried to escape in the shape of this venomous question. I knew, too, it was harder to shape certain words and give them sound in the mouth than to shape their separate letters and write them.

Mammy's face lost colour beneath its hospital pallor and the skin drew tighter. She closed her eyes; the breathing tube gurgled in time with the rapid rise and fall of her chest. She looked again at the slate, then, inch by slow inch, pulled up its transparent plastic cover-sheet. The stylus raced to shape Mammy's speeding copperplate cursive. It was as if she had held the answer captive for fifty years and had been waiting for that key question to free it. She passed the slate back to me.

"His name is Philip Duchamp."

I read the slate, read it again, absorbing the words: Philip Duchamp. My father's name. Words I had never heard spoken, or seen written before, had, just by being there, snuffed out the me I thought I was and left a me that I did not know. The letters blurred and blended as I looked at them. I saw my hand hovering over the words. I wanted to touch them, to claim them, but I could not bring myself to do so. I handed back the slate, handed back the words. Mammy pulled up the clear sheet. I saw the letters, the words, pulling apart, being ripped apart like a scab from a wound. I felt the peeling of it as if it was my own skin with a wound too raw to lose its scab so soon. But the letters that had shaped his name were no more; there was just a clear sheet awaiting a new imprint.

"I was twenty when we met and fell in love."

Twenty? Only? I was born when she was twenty-five. Five years – a long time between them meeting and my birth. Why so long? Was it a happy romance or one that was fraught, I wanted to know, but I didn't ask; somehow, I didn't want to prompt her to tell her story my way. Instead I handed back the slate for her to say more, to say what she wanted to say.

"When he knew that I was expecting you, he wanted to marry me."

But I knew that hadn't happened. No one ever married her. Not him, my father, nor the father of my siblings, either. I glanced over at Mammy. Her eyes were closed. She looked at peace, as if the letting-go of this half-century-held secret had brought her release. How could she be looking relieved and calm when she had visited such turmoil on me? It was not enough; I wanted her to do more, say more. I wanted to shake her up, make her accountable. The stylus carved the words.

"What happened?"

"His family thought he would get kept back in life by me and a child. They sent him away to study. You were born after he left."

So, there were grandparents I never knew who didn't want my

mother; a father who, caving in to his parents' ambitions for him, had left a pregnant girlfriend to go abroad.

"Where is he now?"

"He died. A long time ago. You were away. I heard he had a heart attack."

He had been alive to me for only a minute and already he was dead. But I still wanted more of him. I wanted to know what his life had been like, what paths he had taken after he and Mammy parted – what he did, where he lived and with whom.

"Did he ever marry?"

"He married someone suitable to his family when he qualified, an educated woman from a well-off family."

So, his parents had had their heart's desire – a good match for their bright son. Did they also have that other wish of parents for their children?

"Did they have children?"

She looked up at me after reading my question, and for the first time I saw a look of something like grim satisfaction play over her face.

"No, none."

I turned away from Mammy toward the wall of glass that overlooked the hospital helipad. A waiting helicopter started up, its blades semaphored, "No, none, no, none, nonone, nononenononenonone…" I was the only child of my father, who was now dead, yet he never knew me, nor I him. How could he allow himself to not know his only child? How could he not care what happened to me? I did not want a father who had discarded me before I was born, abandoned me afterwards and had then died without even knowing his only hope of continuance after the grave. Did it not bother him that somewhere there was his living spawn, his child, a stranger? He knew of me as a real person; I did not even have suspicions of him as a possibility, at least not until I had grown up and started to look at and listen more closely to my world. Then I had begun to decode the questions and suggestions, hints and innuendos, which as a child I did not catch.

Complete strangers, meeting us four children together, would sometimes ask in that tactless way we people have, "All you sisters?" and at a nod or a yes, would continue, "Same mother,

127

same father?" which, on being met with an assertive, "yes," would draw a smirk. Some would even persist, "How come she (my) hair so hard and all you (my sisters) own so soft?" With seeds of doubt like this planted, how could I not have guessed that Pappy was not my real father, or at least wondered? I began to unearth buried memories from my childhood.

There was the Saturday morning when I was about ten. Uncle Francois and I were cycling back from a delivery to a florist downtown. The three Peace rosebuds the flower-shop lady had rejected as too open were in my handlebar basket. We were just going past the Registry Building when Uncle Francois dropped his usual loud conversation voice to an urgent, unsettling whisper.

"That's your father behind us."

I looked round for Pappy, didn't see him and whispered back, "Where?"

"Look, he just passed in that big black car. Look, is him, see? He brown, just like you."

I saw a big black chauffeured car ahead. I saw a grey and white head of curly hair, a brown neck and a white shirt collar through the back window. I didn't see Pappy. How could Uncle Francois say that Pappy was in the car? But he seemed so sure. I remember that, at the time, I had shivered as if a ghost had just walked on my grave. I remember, too, that I hadn't said anything then, hadn't asked him to explain. Somehow the whispering had made the whole event confidential – something I should be ashamed and secretive about. He didn't have to say, *Don't tell anyone*; I just knew. We never talked about that incident; it was as if it had never happened.

If that person really was my father, why hadn't he claimed me? What was wrong with me that he didn't want me? He had no other child who could claim a father's love, yet he didn't invest any of his life and love in me. I looked at the slate in my hand. I just couldn't use it any more; its treacherous plastic face, which adopted and discarded with such indifference, could not convey my true feelings of disappointment, of vexation. I had to use my voice, say it out loud. I turned towards Mammy.

"Did my real father ever see me?"

128

She signalled for the slate.

"Once, when you were twelve. I took you to see his mother and he was there."

It came, an entombed memory, resurrected, about a night, a long ago night, when Mammy had told me to put on my Sunday dress and Sunday shoes and socks because we were going out.

"You want me to help the others to dress too?" I had offered.

"No, it's just the both of us."

I remembered Mammy, silent and distracted, plaiting my hair, putting in the white satin ribbons that matched my dress, checking that the bow at the waist was tied to her satisfaction, making me sit while she was getting herself ready; both of us going to a strange car waiting round the corner and heading downtown, pushing open a gate and going up some steps to a gallery, and a woman getting up from a bentwood rocker and leading us to a bedroom, to a bed where an old lady lay.

It had come to my childish mind that the old lady made as little impression on the sheet that covered her as the smallest twigs on the guava tree in the yard at home made on the sky that covered it. I could see again the old lady turning her face to us as we entered the room and her hollowed eyes, bright and searching, peering closely at me as if looking for a sign, and then letting her hand reach from under the covering sheet and Mammy taking my hand and putting it in the old lady's hand, which felt as dry, as curled, as fragile, as a fallen guava leaf. And the old lady pulling me close and looking more intently now, and signalling to the other woman who, coming over to her and moving aside the nightgown neckline so we could see, under the nightie tucks, a wide, white bandage across her bosom, and me, not knowing what that was about and not having enough sense to even guess or ask. And I, suddenly sensing a watching presence, looked up at that very moment through an open door, and caught a glimpse of the shadow of another person in a room beyond, ducking behind a hanging mosquito net.

"Why didn't he want me?"

"He did later on, but it was too late. Pappy had already taken you as one of his own. Your real father saw he had lost his right to you."

129

I read and passed back the slate.

"Pappy loved you. He never let me tell you. After he died I still kept my promise."

Mammy's handwriting had become feint, the letters large, barely formed, the lines of script drooped down the writing slate. Her hand was lying limp at her side; her head was turned away. I left Atlanta for home the next day, promising I would be back soon. My mother was already dead when the plane landed in Trinidad.

Time passed and, one day at the Oval, I spotted Michael Duchamp sitting nearby. I had first met him socially many years before, when Mammy was still alive. On that occasion, he had looked at me closely and asked me what my maiden name was. When I told him he had said, "I think I know your family. Are they from Belmont?" Yes, indeed, they were a long-established Belmont family. On the day of the cricket match, I, feeling empowered with my new knowledge, went over to say hello to him in the luncheon interval. He was sitting with a much older man. Michael held out his arms for a hug and introduced his companion to me. "This is my oldest brother, Lennox. Lennox, this is Josephine Morgan. She was Josephine Dumas. She is Thaïs's daughter." He stressed the word *Thaïs*. Lennox stood up, held out his hand and greeted me: "I could not have passed you on the street. I can see a family resemblance." I sat for a while chatting about the match with the two men. All three of us held the secret of our kinship but none of us would declare it. Wanting to test this common but unshared knowledge I steered the conversation back to Michael's introduction.

"Mammy died two years ago."

"I heard that she had cancer," Michael ventured. "She died in the States?"

"Yes, and with the whole family up there, I really feel like an orphan."

At this, I looked straight at both men.

"Well, girl," countered Michael, "life can be hard."

I went back to my seat as the game resumed, trembling with confused emotions. I wasn't sure what I had expected or hoped for in the encounter. I beat up on myself, berating myself for a missed opportunity. Why hadn't I played the innocent, which they clearly thought me to be? Why hadn't I asked Lennox whose family resemblance he had found in my face? Could I have prompted him, an old man, to be incautious and let slip whose it was? If it wasn't Thaïs's, could it be Philip's? Could it be his mother's or a sister's, maybe?

When I left the Oval that day, I vowed I would visit Michael at his restaurant. I would challenge him openly with my knowledge and get him talking about the man who was my real father, to help me know him. That evening, as I copied the restaurant phone number from the directory, I plotted the flow of conversation in my head. I planned to say how glad I was to see him again and to meet his brother. I would say I wanted us to meet to talk about a personal matter. I would agree to whatever date and time he suggested. That night dragged on. I registered each hour on the clock, unable to fall asleep, feeling myself full to exploding with excitement and anxiety. I tried to imagine how he would receive my call and what he would say to me.

Early next morning, I called. His secretary said he was in a meeting and offered to take a message. I heard myself say, "It's all right; I'll try to reach him later." This I never did. Somehow, the moment, the urgency had passed, the balloon of anticipation in my chest had deflated, my courage had drained away.

I let my interest subside, and, for many years afterwards, as I went back to the rhythms and responsibilities of my days, the desire for a father with a history of his own receded, becoming in my memory nothing but a temporary distraction at one period of my life. One morning, I chanced upon the death notices in the newspaper and saw that Michael Duchamp had died. The notice continued "husband of Simone, father of Michael Jr. and Cecile, brother of Lennox, Philip, Rose and Merle, all deceased." The finality of the announcement seeped into me. I thought for a while about what was entirely gone now. I consoled myself that what I had lost, what had been irretrievably erased, was just a mirage, something I had never quite grasped. Not even my mother's written words had left any tangible trace.

For a long while after, when faced with a mirror, I would pick out the forehead and hairline from Thaïs and the eyebrows and nose too. The eyes, the mouth, the jaw came from elsewhere and I looked at those features in me that must have been his and tried to build in the missing forehead and hairline and eyebrows and nose as if assembling an identikit of a suspect in a crime. I began to ascribe my strange secretiveness, my love of books, my delight in solitude and joy in silence to him, as his contribution to who I am. With Thaïs gone, there is no one to ask if this is so. In any case, she knew him only when they were quite young, half the age I was when I first learned of him. Could she have known him any better than I do? Perhaps, at this, her first big disappointment in life, she had simply allowed a scab to grow over her raw wound and carried on with her life with the same determination and finality with which she had erased from the slate her story, my story, on our last day together.

TO-MAY-TO / TO-MAH-TO

You say to-may-to; I say to-mah-to... she sang along with Sinatra while they stood in his kitchen – she rinsing arugula at the sink, he at the stove doing things to fish and pasta. This new twist to her weekends – Saturday mornings she picked him up, they drove to get breakfast, anywhere where there would be sada roti and some filling (not channa, alloo, bhaji, pumpkin or tomato for him, not meat, saltfish nor smoke herring for her) – this new habit of breakfasting with someone in public brought her a feeling of awkwardness. They sat on a bench on the pitch walk and ate and drank – she coconut water, he bottled water – and, while his talk ran from the architecture that faced them across the road, through colonialism to post-colonial neglect of heritage, she looked at the dappled shade of the overhead poui, shape-shifting on the pavement at her feet, breathed in the green-sap scent of freshly cut Savannah grass – the cut pieces, drifting and settling in the pavement cracks and already beginning to parch to straw – at one with the brackish taste of the too young water nut she was sipping.

What did he want to do next? Did he think he could manage Central Market or maybe the Carenage fish depot, or what about just going to Woodbrook for some organic vegetables? Woodbrook it was for arugula and morai and Carenage for small red fish still jumping on the concrete slab. To the vendor, scaling and gutting, he gave terse instructions: leave the back fin on, take off the belly ones, slit right through the lower jaw. He then launched into a lecture on the skeletal anatomy of various species of fish and its relevance to different culinary styles. She cringed as she saw the looks of tolerant amusement the waiting customers exchanged with one another and with the vendor. She concentrated on rummaging through her handbag, feigning deep interest in its humdrum contents. When he had his catch in hand, she took him and his shopping back to his home, helped him unpack and store, then left.

As night was falling, she returned. It was to the place where he had spent all of his Trinidad years, from where he had left as a boy and had returned a man, back to his mother and grandmother, both now long gone. She knew that house as intimately as she knew her round-the-corner childhood home in their old urban neighbourhood. Until the hiatus of forty or so years she had been a daily visitor to his home, and now it seemed she had become so again. She was not sure about this move – she was not now the person she was then, of that she was certain. But, when she thought about him, about what he said, what he did, how he behaved, she decided that he was who he always was, only more so – it was as if the passage of years had served to concentrate him so that he had, in a sense, become his essence. Still, that he continued to live in the same house, the house of his childhood and hers, made her feel she had entered a former life, made her feel girlish again, full of newness and possibility. She could, and did, spring up the steps as if still seventeen, go through the rooms remembering who what where, remarking on the few changes, the many oh yesses of familiarity. The gallery was almost the same, save that a daybed had replaced the old couch; the two armchairs of the fifties – Danish vogue – occupied their original spaces. The long living space was now one of his main workspaces; every table, chair, surface bristled with his equipment and materials. Under these were stacks of acid-free cardboard boxes full of cleaned, sorted and filed negatives of his early work.

Books on art, history, philosophy, photography filled four bookcases and spilled in multiple awkwardly balanced piles on to the round centre table that she recognised from his mother's Morris set. At first she had thought it was chaotic, but he would mention some idea in a conversation and dart inside and bring out a reference book, plucked from some place that he alone could find. It seemed to her that he had filed in his head every book he owned, and where it was and who had borrowed it and who had returned it, or not. Do you know the work of so-and-so? he would ask. Almost invariably, her lips would form into a moue of regret and he would dash to a bookshelf, push along the exposed spines, snatch out one or two volumes of some person's work, hurry back to her while leafing through them and drop them on her lap, which she would idly flick through to gather a fleeting impression of whatever forceful point he was making about selectivity of subject, subtlety of light, Barthes and Foucault on state-imposed punishment, the ubiquity of Shakespeare in the quotidian, Victorian cooking techniques, pornography versus eroticism.

These forays into the world of the intellect made her feel that she was on the cusp of adulthood once more, with a world to learn about, and privileged to have such erudite access to it. And how he seemed to enjoy being her guide – she was the one with the paper qualifications, he was the one with knowledge. He never tired of showing her this. He had never gone to a university, he proclaimed with pride, dismissing her years at such institutions, so everything he knew he'd learned the hard way. He'd had to ask questions about everything and find the answers for himself, so what he knew, he knew. He knew its mother and father and grandparents and godparents too.

She walked through room after room with the reverence reserved for art galleries or museums. Mounted and framed photos and paintings of his and of fellow artists covered every wall. As in any gallery, the exhibits were changed and rearranged – a work in progress, ha-ha – he declared, with a wide sweep of his arms. Two fish photos of his complemented the fish by a well-known watercolourist friend; cricket of his, the cricket of two other artists; rolling landscapes redolent with history and prom-ise, dancers, carnival masqueraders, steelbandsmen, a rippling muscular male back, an enigmatic child, a self-assured fashion model, a swirling skirt, the back of a head, an embracing couple, flying dreadlocks, blurred fingers percussing on drum skins – in room after room after room. There'd be disconcerting eyes in the bathroom one week, a luscious Cupid's bow pair of parted red lips the next. She would pause respectfully at each in turn while he stood nearby. She felt uneasy, she sensed he was waiting to measure and judge the erudition of her comments, so she made few. Better to be silent and thought stupid, than to speak and remove any doubt. Lovely, lovely, she thought to herself, but where are the pictures of real people – snapshots of friends and family?

The first time she revisited his kitchen she was struck by how little she recognised it. No longer would his mother's mundane pelaus, sancoche and souse come from there. Now, heavy cast-iron skillets and cooking pots hung from angled nails driven into the woodwork. Strainers, pot spoons, spatulas, graters, chef's knives and a sharpening steel framed the Demerara window, on the outside of which rested the stainless steel kitchen sink with its heaped-high draining board of jumbled mugs, plates, bowls, cutlery, pots, storage containers. An old wooden table supported a marble slab with down-turned whisky and wine glasses, a bottle of Campari, several tonic and club soda bottles, a bottle of Talisker. Oh woe – he exclaimed in camp distress one evening – I can't get Lagavulin. An old-time vendor's sloping-sided wooden tray, formerly home to aniseed, mauby bark, cinnamon scrolls, nutmeg, mace and cloves, now overflowed with packets of pills, opened boxes of medications and half-folded sheets of drug manufacturers' crimp. Stacked bowls and plates, bottles of olive oil and balsamic vinegar elbowed cooking wine, salt, pepper mills; below was stowed a bag of Whiskas. If they didn't get that brand they preferred to starve, he confided. Then, bending to place his hands along the backs of the two ultra-discerning felines slithering round his ankles, he addressed them, Don't you my lovelies?

In his mother's mahogany, glass-fronted cabinet, the relics of her once-precious dishes and glasses mingled with his own collection of curios and artefacts of silver and china of different ages, provenance and styles, picked up at random flea markets, second-hand shops, sales, bazaars. Had she ever seen anything as beautifully crafted as this – holding up for her inspection a little silver salt & pepper shaker – late eighteenth century, when people had breakfast in bed with valet, butler and all in attendance. This said with a smile, as if it were a personal reminiscence.

She did not invite him to her home. He spoke so disparagingly about people, like herself, who had fled confined urban spaces for suburbs in other valleys, to estates of identikit "houses built of ticky-tacky". But though she shied away from returning his hospitality, she knew the security of anonymity of place could only be short-lived in such a small country. One day he called to say he was in the neighbourhood and asked if he could drop by. It would have been churlish to make an excuse and refuse. When he got there she could not offer, as he could in his home, "yerba mate from Argentina, jasmine from China or black Russian". Her eyes followed his mute appraisal of her space. The neat row of jars – Lipton's Yellow Label, Twining's Earl Grey, the tin of Svelty powdered milk, the canister of sugar – stowed neatly by size on a shelf under the cupboards did not escape his sweeping eye. She saw him glance at the crowded display of framed snapshots of people he didn't know – multiple pictures of ages and stages of her three children, their spouses, the grandchildren; and single pictures of two he knew – her husband, her mother.

With her eyes downcast, she saw *his* flicker without comment over the only display that would speak to him of her creativity: hand-assembled mobiles of beach stones collected from Baracoa, Rampanalgas, and Macqueripe in shades of grey – slate to ash – coarse to smooth, flattened to rounded, strung together and suspended on fishing wire against a white textured wall hanging. The clay handprints and footprints of her babies, her vases, her straw place mats, her stack of matching tea trays, her little uniform hanging wire baskets vivid with bougainvillaea, her pair of flanking pots overflowing with yellow allamanda, and the stiffly vertical white frangipani bred for suburban gardens came under his silent scrutiny. She could see him assessing how unsophisticated her taste must be. Although he said nothing then, she could see that everything, all that was dear to her, was dwarfed in his eyes when set against his consciously eclectic blue half drum fecund with mixed basils or the coal pot of periwinkle, the mossy clay pots of michaelmas daisies and chrysanthemums, the conch shell of mint which, in his front yard, rested on a strip of rescued fretwork atop an old rusted Singer sewing machine found abandoned in a winding Belmont cul-de-sac. In her own gallery sat the cast-iron frame of her mother's Singer, which she had had carefully cleaned, painted matt black and newly surfaced with plate glass topped by a glazed pot of maidenhair fern. Such cliché middle-class taste.

When she cooked at home, it was usually partially husked brown rice and curried vegetables – basic, frugal sustenance. In his kitchen, he dropped farfalle into boiling salted water with a running commentary – the packet says eight minutes, I prefer seven and a half… You can't get proper rock salt anywhere here… Look what I have to resort to – he indicated a blue canister of what in her kitchen would be special-occasion sea salt. In a deep blue and white authentic Delft dish – one dollar fifty cents in a Toronto flea market, said in a confidential whisper as if the vendor was nearby and could inflate the asking price on learning of his delight at it – he combined butter, olive oil, full-cream milk, crumbled goats cheese. Hmm – he rhapsodised as he decanted the drained, perfectly al dente pasta into the sauce – I've had feta in three continents, even the artisanal product in Greece and, as I was telling my friend Lindy in Austria when we Skyped last week, none is better than the one from Tobago. He stirred in raw chopped arugula, chive, chadon bene and basil. He pan-grilled whole fish – You must sear for four minutes and a half each side… The inside flesh should still be translucent when it is put on the warmed plate… it will continue cooking. She insisted that hers be opaque. Overcooked! A travesty! was his verdict. Only once did she offer him something she had prepared – her signature dip of aubergine and yogurt. He had a spoonful on a Crix in her presence. I would have made it slightly less acid, he pronounced. A week later, she rescued from his fridge her tiny blue and white Corningware dish, still full – bar that single spoonful – of now crusted, weeping baba ganoush. She didn't tell him.

He served the meal at the stove, on his mother's floral deco-rated, gilt-edged Royal Doulton plates. In the gallery, they feasted royally. I cook simply, just ordinary things – brushing aside her compliments – this is how I live; hmmm, it can do with a little of this – shaving Romano from the block over her plate and his. He taught her how to inhale the Talisker and let it vaporise in her mouth – you must chew it! He winced when she said she preferred Campari and coconut water.

After dinner, he insisted that the dishes be left lying just where they were. To clear up now, he declared, would change the mood from enjoyment to work. So she reclined on the daybed surrounded by the remains of the meal while he stretched out there too, his head in her lap. She undid the elastic around his ponytail and released his fine hair, as soft as it ever was, though then, all those decades ago, she hadn't known, hadn't thought to describe in her head, the feel of his hair. She moved her fingers from scalp through the silver cascade, right to the curling tips and back again. He hugged her round her hips and sighed.

– Why won't you make an honest man of me?

She didn't answer – the question was merely self-indulgent, a chance to turn a fine phrase, no more. He was counting on her to note the quality of the question and not put a literal interpretation on it. He continued.

– I was thinking about your house…

He moved his arms from around her and folded them across his chest.

– It's so… suburban… so… sterile…

Her hands slowed their movement through his hair as she waited for him to say more.

– Like… how to put it?… It's like a shrine to your dead husband's ghost.

She did not stop the stroking. It helped her mind to drift away, into a far space where his voice seemed remote. He tilted his head back so that she could see his upside down face.

– You're not answering… You're not saying anything.

Still she didn't answer and, resettling into his former position, he went on.

– If we were to get together, there would have to be some changes. The walls are all white. And those landscapes… those watercolours. You have only fiction on your bookshelves… endless prints of that architect's cityscape sketches.

Here he paused and looked at her with his upside down face again. She did not meet his eyes as he went on.

– Don't you find it static?

When he stopped, his words that she had allowed to fade into the background came into sharper focus. He was talking about her home, her sanctuary, she realised, and not in a nice way. She suddenly felt a surge of longing to be there, with the familiar mundaneness of her bookshelves loaded with fiction and her suburban flowers and the snapshots of her ordinary life. Static security was what she craved, right at that moment. I must go now. She sat up, guiding his head off her lap. Sorry about not helping with the dishes. I don't want to be out driving too late.

She was already opening her car door when his voice drifted down from the top of the gallery steps. Call me when you get home. She didn't answer and when she got home, she didn't call. She was propped up in bed, her own queen-sized bed with floral sheets and matching big pillows, reading, rereading, a short story collection, *May We Borrow your Husband? and Other Comedies of the Sexual Life*, an old favourite by a beloved old favourite and had just started the story, "Cheap in August", when the phone shrilled in her ear. His number came up and she thought he might be calling to confirm she had got home safely. Her upbeat hello was met by a deep hiss from his end.

– Are you back in your smug, comfortable life?

She sat up straight. Where had that come from? What had prompted that? It was as if a gecko she was holding in her palm had morphed into a scorpion.

– Do you ever think about what you did to my life?

His voice was grating, low, as if it came from his deepest viscera. She pictured him lying in his bed, head sunk into his pyramid of pillows, comforter drawn up to his chin.

– You listening? Yes, I want you to listen. I want you to think about how I felt all those years, forty-four years! Catching glimpses of you with… with… *that… person*. A comfortable life, you say, a home and children and being Mistress So-and-so. That person who came from nowhere decided what kind of life I was to have. I had plans. We had plans. But that counted for nothing. In the end, I got nothing.

She said to herself, though she knew she should say it aloud to him but couldn't. Nothing? So, whose are the lips, the breasts, the eyes, the legs, the feet, the buttocks, the hands, the pubes that hang from your walls in colour, in stark black and white? What of the girl who, you report, passing by a Tobago fisherman's beach stall, reached out, pulled the pulsing heart right out of a flapping cavali and popped it in her mouth – at which the fisherman, jaw open, could only say, Where you from girl? What of the intellectuals of the left bank of sixties barricaded Paris and the slumming aristocratic babes of swinging London? Don't say you got nothing.

The sting had stopped hurting; now she was numb. She put the phone handset on the bedside table, from where it continued to drone, his voice reduced to a distant irritated static. She slid back down to her semi-reclining reading position and picked up her Graham Greene... *When it came to the decision there seemed nothing to choose except red snapper and tomatoes and again she offered him her tomatoes; perhaps he had grown to expect it and already she was chained by custom...* She let him unburden on the phone, well past midnight, and off and on she listened. He did not expect anything from her but murmurs of agreement, grunts of admission – the aural and oral equivalent of breast-beating. She couldn't hang up – what anger would she be penting up in him to be later unleashed on herself by that act? She couldn't defend herself – what defence could she have against the accusation that she had deliberately sabotaged his life? She had once said she knew what she was doing when she got married, he accused. She hadn't done it without careful thought. That night he persisted with that theme.

– Did you even for a minute think about me? Did you remember me? Maybe you did and decided that I was of no value; I could be dispensed with like that.

The dismissive finger and thumb click came clear down the phone line. What was the honest answer to that? What was the safe answer? The honest answer was not the safe answer. The former would ignite a firestorm; the latter couldn't be supported by her actions in the past. She decided she couldn't make an honest man of him until she became an honest woman herself, and that was more than she could bear to contemplate. Honesty, she had long decided, was somewhat overrated as a virtue – used by those who didn't want the hard work that goes into what was, to her, a nobler virtue, charity. She said to him, aloud, I thought of you and hoped you were happy too. She listened. There was no answer. Good night, she said and again listening, again heard nothing. She hung up, rolled onto her right side, read a few more lines: "*I always sleep*

141

well." It was a lie – the kind of unimportant lie one tells a husband or a lover in order to keep some privacy... She closed her eyes and waited for a fine, deep sleep.

MAKING PASTELLES IN DICKENSLAND

I didn't stop to think. I just blurted out what jumped into my head.

"You serious? With all that is happening right now, you talking about making pastelles?"

"But, I really want to make pastelles," he said.

"Here?"

"Yes."

True, it was December, and what is that month for if not to set grated ginger, cloves, cinnamon and water in an earthenware jar out in the hot sunshine to concentrate their spicy zing, separate blood-red sorrel sepals from their fat, spiky seed pods and brew from them a tart ruby beverage; pack all manner of minced dried fruit into tall glass jars to soak in rum for the black fruit cake. And above all, what was December for, if not to make pastelles? But that was another time – another life.

We made pastelles on the weekend before Christmas. Early on the Saturday morning, he took the cutlass to the lush grove of banana trees that sprang out of the compost heap in the backyard. I looked down from the kitchen window, now and again catching sight of his wide-brimmed West Indies cricket hat as the broad blades of the banana trees fanned the angled sunlight, first lighting then shadowing him. He chose only perfect leaves – smooth, entire, not yet ravaged by time into ragged ribbons. The night dew, bright crystal balls, caught the blue sky and raced off the slick surface of the leaves, whole worlds of fortune spinning away. He held up the cut leaves, each big enough to screen all six-foot of him, and every time he was lost to view, I could feel my breath stop a little, till I caught sight of him again. With the care of one putting a sleeping baby in its cot, he laid the leaves one over one to build a pile, a dozen leaves high. He then ran the blade along the midribs. From the midribs a grating shriek rose as weft and warp parted, and the half leaves curled away from the blade, green waves breaking on the lawn sea.

Then, I would go down to take him a drink of iced water in his Ddraig Goch tankard. As he turned towards me, I crossed my fingers to protect my good fortune. How lucky I was to have found him – an unexpected gift. How lucky that he left his own big country to live in mine, to make my little Caribbean island his. He smiled, sweat channelling down his face. He drained the tankard in long gulps. I stroked his cheek with the back of my hand; he bent his head and leaned into the touch. His shoulder was warm, sinewy through the thin, damp T-shirt; his thick brown mane fell over his eyes screening their green depths. He lifted the half-leaves and draped them across my outstretched arms, chief celebrant to acolyte, and I took them to the kitchen, to the hot work of tearing them into squares, softening them over a flame, transforming them from crisp and brittle to limp and pliable. I could hear him calling the children over from the swings where they were waiting until this moment, when, with no cutlass flailing the air, it was safe. I watched as they played with the heap of pale midribs, catching glimpses of the make-believe spears fletched with clinging leaf remnants, fluttering like festive bunting as they sailed towards their target – the wrinkled trunk of the big old flamboyant. High-pitched screeching, the soft patter of barefooted running mingled with the deep, "careful" or "well-done" and the clomping of wellingtons, floated up to the kitchen.

But that was then.

"Yes," he said again, "couldn't we?"

"And where will we find banana leaves in Southwark?"

"We don't have to use banana leaves. We can use aluminium foil. People do that nowadays, you know, even back home."

"My mother would turn in her grave."

It was only an excuse, I knew. I couldn't voice the thought that he wasn't up to doing anything that called for much effort. Even getting ready to leave the house that morning would have taken twice as long as it did, if the others – our adult children – hadn't been there to help. We talked as we walked the short distance to the train to take us to his last radiotherapy before the Christmas weekend. He held my arm, holding me close as if I was the one needing support. I cursed the cold air that bit through dense wool layers – coat, scarf, jumper, vest, and trousers – into bones. I cursed the ice-slicked pavement. I cursed the disease that was chewing him up from inside. He did not complain nor did we speak about his condition. Speaking it, the implications of it, would make it real – something to contend with.

At the hospital, I sat on a chair of sterile moulded plastic, a body-sized heap of shed outer garments on the chair beside me, as I looked through the plate glass at him, at what they were doing to him. They fitted the plastic bivalve shell, a mould of his head, over his face and closed it shut, trapping him, holding his skull fast in place, so that the rays could target and burn out the cells that had spread through the interstices – wherever lymph flows. I could see him tensing, fighting the claustrophobia that kept him out of elevators and closed rooms. My stomach squeezed acid bile up my throat as I watched his struggle with himself behind the mask.

Afterwards, in the hospital canteen, we had weak, acrid tea in small paper cups, just to do something ordinary, though neither of us could manage even that mean cupful. We gathered our scarves and gloves, shook on our coats and stumbled into the sleety rain to fight for a cab, losing over and over to the more agile, the fitter and healthier. On the way back we sat, propped up against each other. I rested my head on his shoulder and through his coat, his jacket, his shirt, I could feel bones – bones laid bare – the sharp outline of the joint where arm bone fitted into shoulder socket, every movement now amplified. We hardly spoke, but I wouldn't let go of his hand, the skin cold, clammy, translucent, a fragile shield to his long, thin finger bones. We emerged into a veil of sunset-gilded fog that blurred the edges of everything, softening the view. He shivered and I reached up to pull the knitted hat over his ears. The corners of his lips lifted in a grateful smile, and I ran a finger along a new deep groove in his greyed face, thinking that it was only six months ago that I could barely keep up with him when we went on evening walks through our old neighbourhood. Now, he put his arm around my shoulder, slowing my pace to match his – his way, I thought, of slowing down time.

I was grateful for the fog. It quickly absorbed the noise and reek of traffic from the main road just behind us. We entered a ghostly realm away from reality, a dream space where our shoes made no sound on the cobbles of the narrow lane, where neither buildings nor worries seemed to have a discrete form. The things inside me were hard and weighty but had no shape and no names. I had no way of saying those things to myself in my own head and no way of saying them aloud. I did not know then, though I think I know now, that hard things have no words for them – they are too heavy to float up and out of the mouth; they stay stuck inside and, around them, lighter things rise up, bubbles that float free. It was easier to make out that we were in an ordinary, everything-is-all-right world.

"Isn't this little area so like a back-in-time place?"

"It's surprising really, that it is still here. Most of the bombing was just there, along the docks, the warehouses and so on." He gestured towards the river.

"Quite a miracle then that this little Victorian bit escaped. It's so quaint."

"Yes, it's like it's not real."

"I looked it up on the A-Z before I came. I was charmed by the street names."

"Check this one – Copperfield Street." He pointed to a street sign set into the wall of a building, hazy in the fog.

"And I spotted a Little Dorrit Park nearby. I wonder whether parents who take their children there to play think about Little Dorrit's ghost?"

"Marshalsea Road makes me look over my shoulder for Fagin."

"You know he lived round the corner? In Lant Street."

"Who? Fagin?" He squeezed my arm as he said this.

"No, clown. Dickens." I looked at his face and we smiled. "You know what? I'm really looking forward to reading something about the history of this place – stuff like whether Dickens' fiction was used to name the places or whether the real places found their way into the fiction."

"What I'm looking forward to right now is a lie down and a cup of real tea."

We arrived and opened the door to warmth and cosiness, to the promise of rest and tea.

Later that evening we six gathered for dinner. The talk ran to Christmas preparations.

"Your father wants pastelles." I raised my eyes to heaven.

"Yum! Pastelles!"

"Wouldn't be Christmas otherwise."

"Tomorrow. We can make them tomorrow."

"What about the cornmeal?" I wondered whether no one but me was grounded in reality.

"We sure to find cornmeal somewhere."

The next morning we found no cornmeal in Southwark, but in nearby Elephant & Castle, a Colombian shop stocked raw cornmeal of a coarse variety. It was that or nothing, and the one thing it couldn't be was nothing. His smile lifted his thinned face – he had had a triumph, something was working out. We bought the other ingredients, and by the time we were done, he had to be helped down the steps for he was in a cold sweat and limp. We stood by the curb with the creeping realisation that London's iconic taxis did not frequent Elephant & Castle. At a minicab outlet they promised us a cab in half an hour. On the cold, damp steps of the shopping centre, he sat huddled in the gloomy mizzle of the day as the half hour lengthened. Standing apart, pacing the pavement, I could feel my irritation at this whimsical enterprise rising. Why had we willingly chosen to subject ourselves to this misery? We could all have stayed home, warm and snug. When finally we got back to the house, it took a couple of hours before mint tea with honey and bed rest did their work and he could stand without help.

We crowded into the tiny kitchen. I looked on as they poured the cornmeal into a wide bowl, worked in salt, a big knob of butter.

"Mummy, how much water?"

"Start with two cups." The dough remained stiff, too brittle to shape.

"Drizzle in some water till it's softer."

A drizzle – nothing; another – nothing; a third and suddenly the mass loosened, slumping to a yellow puddle.

"Water more than flour." Our metaphor for total disaster popped into my head; I tried to shut it out by closing my eyes to its literal manifestation.

Ordinarily, to return it to the right state, we would just add more cornmeal. But how could we do that? We had just used it all up. It was late. Elephant & Castle would be closed for the night.

"Try dusting on some regular flour to help it bind," he suggested.

A quick check was made of the cupboards.

"Sorry, can't see any."

"You know what? Let's just stop now. It's not going to work." I tried to get them to see sense.

"Come on, let's at least get some flour and see if that works." He wouldn't give up.

There was a hurried trip to the corner shop.

A fine rain of white flour was sifted over and the dough kneaded till it was smooth. I prodded the mass with a judgmental finger. The dough sank then bounced back.

"Just look at this. This is too springy for pastelles. I start to make pastelles and now I find myself making cornmeal dumplings."

I could hear my voice coming out thin, whiny, complaining.

They persisted.

"I like dumplings."

"Me, too."

"Me, three."

"Stuffed cornmeal dumplings? That could become the new signature dish."

So much effort, so much making do, for what? I just wanted it to finish, to be done with, no matter how it turned out.

"OK, just do whatever you want."

They took over.

"I will make the dough into balls while you cook the meat."

"Put plenty seasoning, you hear? Pepper, herbs."

"I'm going to chop the olives."

"Can somebody get out the raisins and capers and put them in little dishes?"

"Daddy, would you like to sit here and cut the foil?"

Back home, he manned the wooden press. Taking a piece of banana leaf, placing it on the press, dipping his fingers into a bowl of olive oil and running them over the leaf, placing a cornmeal ball on the greased leaf and patting it flatter, greasing a second leaf, placing it on the ball, folding the hinged upper half of the press with its long arm over the lot, applying pressure on the arm to flatten the ball, reversing the action with the press, lifting the top leaf to reveal a perfect, thin disc on the bottom leaf: all this took under a minute. In Dickensland there was no pastelle press, so what could we use?

"What about a rolling pin?" I asked.

"We don't have one."

"An ordinary rum bottle?"

"A rum bottle isn't ordinary here, Mummy."

"Any kind of bottle?"

We looked at the available alcohol bottles – square section, embossed, tapering, bulbous – whatever happened to cylindrical as the basic bottle shape? A trip out was made again – this time a quest for a suitable bottle.

We laughed at the report that came back. "The barman at the pub couldn't believe I was choosing alcohol according to the shape of the bottle it was in. He asked if it was for some kind of ritual."

We now had a bottle of vodka for a pastelle press. I looked across at him. He was sitting up straight and rubbing his palms together. He looked as boyish and as eager as he did when we first met more than thirty years before. My irritation evaporated in the warmth of his smile, his delight in anticipation. He was about to engage in something that gave him pleasure, something he had set in motion and was about to see to its satisfying finish. He oiled two squares of foil, placed the dough ball on one, flattened the ball slightly, placed the second square on top, and rolled the bottle from the centre outwards till the ball was flattened. He then lifted a corner of the top foil square to separate the two foil pieces. Six heads bent over the counter to witness the result. Each piece of foil bore ragged pieces of flattened dough. There was no perfect disc. We looked at one another, trying to find a way to make it work.

"Let's roll it back in a ball and try again, only, don't press so hard."

This time, almost all stayed on the bottom foil, but it wasn't flat enough or big enough.

"Let's try with just the bottle and the bottom foil."

The dough wrapped itself firmly around the bottle and wouldn't peel off in one piece.

"Cling film, try cling film."

"But you can't steam pastelles in cling film." My voice was raised more than I had intended. I could see them looking at one another in a sort of helpless way. He spoke softly.

"I know. You're right. But we can try to roll it out between pieces of cling film and transfer it to the foil afterwards for filling and cooking."

They were all looking at me, urging me to go along. Why were they doing this? Making me feel bad, as if I was being difficult. We had created this problem ourselves; why? Surely we had enough to deal with already. Was I the only one who could see that?

Prising the roll of cling film from the box, I scratched and scratched and scratched around the whole circumference, trying to find the end of the roll and finally I found something that was a possibility. I traced it around and started pulling a good length. With the roll now back in the box, I was ready to tear the film against the serrated metal strip. The piece that I had pulled away from the roll flipped over, making of itself a thick creased ribbon. I tore it off and started to unfold it. It first clung to my palm then fell back, folding on itself again. I crumpled the scrap and started over, found the end once more and unrolled a smooth length, pulling it against the sharp edge of the box. But instead of cutting cleanly, the film gathered into a ruffle, trapped in the metal teeth. Snatching the bad-minded, stupid little piece of thing, I crumpled it too. I searched around the roll to find the end again. It seemed that all eyes were fixed on my hands fumbling at the simple task. I stopped and looked at what I was fighting with – a silly little roll of plastic film – and losing. I could feel my eyes fill up, my throat get tight. The roll of cling film was still in my hands. I held it firmly and twisted my hands round and round until the cardboard tube was a warped spiral and I hurled the damn thing against the kitchen wall.

Hands fidgeted. Feet shuffled. No one spoke. They looked at one another and slipped out of the kitchen, leaving us two alone. The tears spilled out and ran hot and salty down my face. He looked up, holding out his hand to me and when I took it, he pulled me to him, to where he was seated. He put his arms around my hips. He rested his head on my chest, smothering his face between my breasts as I stood close in at his chair. I cradled his head in my arms. Glancing over his head I could see the blurred words I could chant by heart, "*Prednisolone, allopurinol, ondansetron, ranitidine*" – words written with care on a hand-drawn chart stuck on the fridge behind his chair, his neat red check marks alongside days of the week and frequency of dosage – as if by doing his best with the writing he would be investing in a karma that would make the drugs do their best too. I lifted the end of my jumper to wipe away the tears as they fell on his bare scalp – his hair had been lost months before. Spinal chemotherapy, long needles pumping toxic chemicals into the marrow of his spine, over and over, had further delayed regrowth. His juddering sobs shook my belly. I sat on his lap. His legs were thin bamboo sticks through the fabric of his trousers. Our heads nested on each other's shoulder, mine on his, his on mine. I could feel his heart throbbing through his chest and mine; I was sure he could feel mine too. How did we get to this?

The disease had crept up on him, feigning a flu that wouldn't leave, then wasn't flu any more, but a lymphoma too nascent to be treated. "Maybe you'll be ready for treatment in about twenty years or so," they assured. In twenty days, he went into shock as the disease had suddenly become very aggressive. The prognosis remained optimistic.

"He'll be back home for Christmas," from the hospital.

"I'll be back home for Christmas," from him.

November passed, December started. I came instead and found him gaunt, weak and fragile. I saw he was trying for my sake, for all our sakes, to be more than he had become. It was not meant to go like this. There was no plan for this. We were going through a difficult phase, I had told myself, but in the end, all would be well and we would pick up our life where we had left off. I had vowed to myself that I would make it better, would try to be more deserving of the good things I had been gifted with. Now, all that seemed a naïve, foolish bargain. I had clung to an earlier promise of a bone marrow transplant; we were told that it would not, could not, now be done.

There, in the kitchen, with the chaos of unfinished business around us, he patted my back. How many times had I seen him comfort an unhappy child that way?

"We can do this. OK? We can get through this."

I kissed the top of his head.

"Yes. Yes. We can do this."

I stood up, smoothed my hair, splashed my face at the sink and tried to assess where we were and to see what we could salvage of the interrupted pastelle-making session.

He started opening drawers.

"What you looking for?"

"A tablecloth."

The others came back into the kitchen.

"A tablecloth, you said? This is the only one I have."

From a high cupboard came the bright green Breton linen tablecloth, embroidered with black and white, a wedding present of ours that we had given her, our eldest, when she set up her own home.

"But it will be spoilt. Get caked up with dough," I objected.

"Mummy, wasn't it you who told me that we must make use of everything we have?"

She handed him the tablecloth and he spread it on the table.

"Ladies and gentlemen, close your eyes for a minute and imagine this... St James on a Saturday night. Pavement stalls. Tables spread with white sheets for tablecloths. And the vendors rolling out roti after roti after roti. OK? Open eyes now. Here we go."

We laughed at that incongruous image and I could sense the warming of the atmosphere in the room at his little joke. Everyone was trying to pretend that my outburst hadn't happened. I, wanting to make amends by behaving as if nothing was wrong, joined in.

"You think I should light a flambeau? For authenticity?"

He dusted the cloth with flour, gathered up the bits of dough that still clung to the bottle, made a new ball of it, flattened that, laid it on the floured cloth, rubbed flour along the bottle and proceeded to roll out a perfect disc, lifting and turning the dough around until it was as big as a tea plate. The dough behaved. He rolled it over the bottle and flipped it on to a foil square.

"Now, let's start filling and folding."

To the busy sounds of a parang CD, we got into our assembly line while joining in the chorus.

"*Somos caminantes, tenemos que andar.*"

"*We are travellers; we must continue on our journey.*"

First meat, cooked with generous handfuls of fresh herbs, then raisins, olives and capers, the filled discs folded into rectangular packages, wrapped in foil to make twenty-four plump pastelles. Half a dozen at a time were put to steam in a colander over a saucepan of boiling water. The fragrances of home – thyme, garlic, chives – filled the house and he, stretched out on the sofa, caught my eye and winked. We ate pastelles by candlelight, just for the romance of it. They were pronounced delicious. We drank vodka. We talked of Christmases past and of Christmases to come. I warned them that this year they would not get the customary pillowslip stockings from Santa Claus, a tradition that, if they thought about it rationally, they would agree had continued ridiculously long after their childhood was past.

"That's up to Santa Claus surely, not you."

When they became absorbed in a game of backgammon, he and I muffled up to go for a walk. He left his stick behind. We leaned against each other as we stepped into the sharp cold. The drizzly fog had changed to flurries of snow. The black night swallowed all but the feeble streetlights, whose hopeful glow made shifting rainbow haloes through the slowly wafting snowflakes. Cocooned against the cold, we ambled, arm in arm, along Weller and Sturge, Union and Pepper. As we drifted through Dickensland in a Christmas card scene of cobbled streets, softly gleaming windowpanes and snow piled on windowsills, our breaths made floating speech bubbles of our conversation about *Great Expectations* – a conversation about resolute Pip and poor Estella who lost the best gift she was ever given. He and I went on this, our last walk together, discussing lives that were not ours. At the end of that story, Pip and Estella parted, promising to continue as friends apart.

We didn't talk about it, but I think that while we strolled, we were writing our magical end to our own story.

A PERFECT STRANGER

We were not always like this. I mean us, we two. Like this – this one, past the best-before age of three-score and ten; and the other, crystallised dust in a jar, lying in a teak box on the dressing table.

Close your eyes to the sagging skin, the drooping frame, the sparse, man-cut, greying hair and see beneath the girl of twenty-one that you first laid eyes on one Easter weekend, half a century ago, in a granite building atop the hill of a mid-Wales seaside town. And I will see you too, risen from under your blanket of crisp rose petals, faded photographs, curling, grief-filled cards, the yellowing, passionate, desperate notes, written too late.

The first time I saw your face, the world I knew before fell away. I closed my eyes to capture your image, to hold it behind my eyelids, to gaze at it inside my head. I never wanted to lose sight of you ever again.

You remember where we were that day? It was at the men's hall of residence, where, over the four-week Easter break, third-year students, like you, putting in the extra slog before finals, stayed locked into their little cliques of focused swots, away from the aimless overseas students, like me, with nowhere to go in their vacation time, with little to do but drift around the only welcoming space, an open hall of residence, to carry on moaning in an unending circuit of longing about back home in Uganda, back home in Nepal, back home in Trinidad.

Back home in Trinidad was the conversation between the two men and me as we limed in the room of the one who was in his final year – he was later to marry a Welsh girl and stay on; the other was a second-year student, bound for a life of success as a diplomat. When the good-natured teasing about how awkwardly

I was coping with the strangeness around me took on what I felt was a somewhat more judgemental tone, I flung a pillow at one; he retaliated, I flung it back, harder this time, and it quickly became a pillow fight which I was losing. I left the room with a hurt head and even more hurt feelings.

You know something? Many years later, when you were long gone, I was with our son at a post office in Port of Spain and who should come in but the by then retired diplomat who, when introductions were made, said to my son, "If it wasn't for me, you wouldn't be here." At which our son gave me a surprised 'what have you been keeping from me' look and the diplomat seeing his expression, laughed and said, "Don't worry, you're the image of your father. What I meant was, your mother, a friend and I had a fight when we were students and, after she ran away from us, your mother met your father."

I stumbled to the bathroom – communal baths and showers – closed the door to a bath cubicle, sat on the edge of a bathtub and cried. At first the tears were about the fight, about the unfairness – two ganged up against one – then about being away from anyone who belonged to me – no letter from home for a few weeks, then about the disappointment of no daffodils fluttering and dancing beside Windermere where I had just been on a fortnight's geology field trip, and about not being able to go up Scafell with the climbers, and that disappointment merged into feeling wretched about my lack of foresight in failing to book a room for when I returned – it was the Easter weekend and the office of the only hall available was closed for business, so there I was, the unofficial and clandestine guest of those two fellow-Trinidadians with whom I had been stupid enough to pick a fight. Not genteel tears rolling silently along damp cheeks, I was sobbing uninhibitedly – loud and hard, full of rage and self-pity.

"Are you all right?" A man's voice came over the partition wall from the adjoining cubicle.

I hadn't stopped to think about whether I was alone. I caught my breath and strangled a sob before it could come out of my throat. I didn't dare say a thing. There was a silence, too, from the neighbouring cubicle, but I could feel a listening presence. I feared even to breathe, lest my breath made a snuffle that could be heard.

"Are you all right?" Softer now, some uncertainty had edged into it.

I was still silent. I wished the owner of the voice would think he had been mistaken. That he had imagined hearing someone crying. I couldn't leave, I had nowhere to go. I couldn't go back to my friends. I had no room of my own. In the two cubicles, there was a listening silence that lasted many minutes. Then I heard a swishing and splashing noise, bathwater sloshing against the sides of the bath, followed by a loud whoosh and the noise of water falling from a height. I could work out that the person had stood up in the bath and the noise was the water falling off him. The plug was pulled, water gurgled away. Listening hard I picked up noises like a body being rubbed dry and the slap of slippers on the tiled floor. I heard the click of a bolt being pulled and felt relief; I was certain that my neighbour would just mind his own business and go away. The rap at my cubicle door was soft, but I was startled and didn't answer.

"You're not going to do anything you will regret, are you?"

Such worry was in the voice that I had to say something.

"No. I'm not."

"Would you like to talk?"

When I opened the door, did I stare at you? You didn't stare at me even though my face was red, eyes red, nose runny, cheeks wet. But could you sense what I was thinking? I think now that you sensed even then that I could love you, a perfect stranger for ever, for you came into the cubicle, closed the door and sat next to me on the edge of the bath. You leaned back, turned on the tap and wet a corner of the towel that you slipped from over your shoulder. You wiped my face with the damp corner and dried it. You sat next to me and asked me nothing. We sat in a long silence. I breathed in a new fragrance from your skin – sandalwood soap, I learned later. I looked down at my hands folded in my lap, at your hands also folded in your lap – long slim fingers, dark hair springing from the backs of your wrists. I looked at your feet, slim and pale in soft, beige felt-looking slippers and at mine, bare and brown, stirrup straps of the chocolate-coloured stretch pants hooked under the insteps. The way you were gave off a sense of security, of completeness, of knowing how to do things the right way, of understanding your world, the one into which I had stumbled, blindfold, picking my way around in error and confusion. I was embarrassed that I had made a fool of myself and had to be rescued. I didn't dare look at you for shame. After a while, you took my hand and said, "Whatever it is, it's not that bad." You were wearing your fawn dressing gown – it served you well for at least a decade more – and from a pocket you took out a black and gold tin of cigarettes. You shook out two. You lit both and passed me one. We sat and smoked. The sweet molasses flavoured Balkan Sobranie calmed and relaxed me. You crushed the glowing gold tips in the lid of the tin, put the blackened stubs in your pocket and closed the tin. You looked into my eyes. I looked into yours for the first time. Green, flecked with gold.

"Are you going to be all right now?"

"Yes."

SIC TRANSIT WAGON

That afternoon a man she guessed to be about her age called at her front gate. "You selling the wagon?" While his question was directed at her, his gaze was not. It was fixed on his cap which he was holding in both hands, turning it around and around. She too looked at the cap and at his hands. They appeared soft, softer than hers, as if they were reserved for dealing only with soft things. A big gold signet ring on the index finger of his right hand made a rhythmic metallic clink against the brass rivets along the edge of the cap – *clink, clink, clink* – like a metronome ticking away the seconds while he waited for her answer.

He was just the latest of the string of people who stopped at the gate, almost every month, ringing the bell, calling out, "Hello?" "Anybody home?" They came in twos – one at the gate, the other waiting in their vehicle. The one at the gate said, "I always passing here and seeing the wagon park up. You selling it?" You would think that hearing that question about a dozen times a year for the past couple years, she had a ready yes or no answer. But she didn't. Because, truth be told, she didn't know from one day to the next, whether the wagon was for sale.

But each time she said, "Maybe –", and the man, always a man, answered, "I could come in and take a look at it?" And she, forgetting that morning's quota of headlines shrieking of kidnapping, murder, rape, burglary said, "OK", and the passenger emerged. The two of them opened the gate, advanced towards the car, opened its doors and bonnet and trunk, tapped roof and trunk door and bumpers and doors; all the while listening, more carefully than her doctor ever did for her bronchial asthma, to determine whether the car was metal, metal and rust or rust and fill. "I could start the engine?" they asked next and, as the key was always in the ignition, they would start it, rev it, checking the exhaust for black smoke and water droplets.

She was quick to point out the car's deficiencies, to discourage them. "The air conditioning doesn't work... look at how much rust on the body... the trunk door won't stay up... no power anything... it's twenty-five years old." They would nod while carrying on with their tapping and tapping.

There was always some story about why they wanted it. It seemed to her that they felt they had to justify their wanting to take the wagon away from her. One older man came barefoot, trouser legs rolled up above his stringy calves, T-shirt neckline ringed dark with sweat and all of him – eyelashes and all – covered with a spray of fine grass cuttings. "This trunk could take mower, bushwhacker, blower, rake, cutlass, gas bottle, everything, easy-easy." Another saw different possibilities in the trunk – packed with the uniformed bodies of primary school children, "I could fit four or five in there, a next four in the back seat – that make it four and four eight, two more in front with me, eight and two is ten – ten at least could transport to school in the morning and home in the evening." One was building a house and could use it to carry blocks, cement bags, gravel; the younger ones were "looking to fix it up" as their first car. One fellow and his partner planned to convert it to a pick-up. "We could get that feller with the welding torch to cut off the top, pull out the back seat and put in two big barrel – we does sell fish." And then the inevitable, "How much you want?" and her ready answer, "How much you offering?" And, no matter what they said, from her came, "Let me think about that. What's your number? I'll call you." And early next day, "No, sorry. I decided to keep it."

Because, truth to tell, the wagon wasn't just a car. It was *her* car – the first car she ever owned. That gleaming silver 1.8 Toyota Corolla station wagon – foreign assembled, imported at a time when most cars were locally assembled – was extra special. "That is one sick car," the boys she taught declared. Oh, yes, she had had cars before – she could claim either of the two in the yard. But this car was the first with her name on the "Certificate of Ownership". It was registered just around the time of her birthday. Your thirties must end with a bang, her still thirty-eight-year-old husband said, presenting her turned thirty-nine gift. She thought of herself as being in her prime of her life, but old, she supposed, to get one's first car. Growing up, she had never even imagined owning a car – nobody she knew owned one. She didn't get around to doing the driving test till, at twenty-seven, she was pressured by her first pregnancy, and it was another decade or so before the big deal of that Certificate of Ownership.

How old were the children then? The oldest, eleven, the middle, seven, the youngest, two. She has a photo of them standing by that new car, the little one sitting on the bonnet, the others standing, flanking, outside the house on the hill where they then lived. She remembers the drama of that picture being taken. Husband, meticulous, in charge of the Canon, arranging the children. By the time he had got the composition just right, they had lost all interest in the proceedings. But they wanted to please, and so they were captured smiling. The eldest, a little apprehensive, the middle one not wanting to be in a picture at all but cooperating to get it over with, the little one happy to be sitting on a car bonnet and having her picture taken.

The wagon transported these three, one neighbour's three, and another neighbour's two to the Botanic Gardens, to school, to parties and to the beach. There were bikes and trikes, kites and balls, flippers and armbands, goggles and masks, swimsuits and wet towels, bats and racquets and kiddies' carnival costumes. Market days saw bags of navel oranges and grapefruit for homemade juices for lunch kits, coconuts for water and sweet-bread, baskets of fruit and vegetables and fish. Pink and blue day-old chicks won at bazaars, guinea pigs, rabbits, tropical fish, baby manicous, budgies, ducks, cats and dogs were moved around in the wagon as were bags of soil and manure, plants, tools, lawn mower and bushwhacker. The back of the wagon was the mobile sixth-form reference library for her subject and, in the El Niño-inflicted drought decades, it served as the family water cart – brined-pig-tail buckets filled daily at standpipes were ferried home for cooking, washing, bathing and flushing.

The wagon taught the two older ones to drive. Those were the happy years, she thinks now. Husband fashioned two squares from a piece of thin ply, sanded the surfaces, rounded the corners, applied one, two, three coats of white gloss enamel paint; on each, drew on an "L" using a ruler, set square and pencil, painted the "L" in red, pierced two holes at the top, ran cutlass wire through the holes, fastened the L plates to the front and rear bumpers, sat in the front passenger seat and invited the eldest to sit in the driver's seat. "But Daddy, I can't drive." "That's true; but you are going to learn." When it was the middle child's turn, his "I'm not going with him" decided that she was the one to fasten the L-plates to the wagon and be the accompanying adult. The youngest turned seventeen on one side of the Atlantic while she and the wagon were on the other, and there was no husband on either side. Ah, yes. But it was the youngest, driving the wagon many years later, who suddenly shouted, "Look, look, look at the dial – 99 996. 9." And she was the one who drove round and round the block to eat up the decimals, slowing down as if running out of gas, eyes on the meter, pulling up, stopping and clapping and shouting, "100000 miles!"

Years before, when they moved to the house where she now lives, the wagon ran shuttle trips, carrying everything. They had lived in the old house for more than two decades and it took six months to leave it with the wagon ferrying between the houses. It would overheat, the needle trembling over the red H zone, enforcing a rest while the engine cooled down, so she could say goodbye to one house and hello to the other. Those were the months when she would feel herself unable to get enough air, and, in the kitchen of either house, she would catch hold of the edge of the sink with both hands, press her fingertips into the cold stainless steel, blanched knuckles straining the skin taut, her thumbs pushing hard against the sink rim. She would cling on to stop herself from falling, from screaming, from disappearing. Unfinished gasping yawns fought against her efforts to get a breath in. Empty! Empty! she would command herself. And she would squeeze her belly muscles and push air out in long slow whooshing exhalations through her nostrils until there was nothing left, and the incoming breath would find her mouth and glide in on its own in hiccupping gasps as she gradually released her belly and eased out the panic attack. She took the wagon to the

162

radiator works and they gave the radiator what she thought of as an acid bath, purge and enema to remove whatever was causing the blockage in its circulation and the needle stayed out of the H zone thereafter. She remembers marvelling at the ease with which mechanical maladies could be remedied.

By the time of the move, the wagon had already taken the first child to the airport after every university holiday and brought her back home at the end of term. A year after the move, the second child followed. Too soon, it would take her mother on her last trip to the airport and her husband on his last journey in Trinidad. She went away then and left the wagon for almost three years, parked and unused on the grass in front of her house. She was shocked on her return to see how subdued it looked, sitting low to the ground. The tyres had been flattened by the weight of the body. The paintwork was no longer bright silver but dull and scabby, mottled grey like leprous skin. The daily roast under the vertical sun had cracked the dashboard plastic and pale foam oozed from cracks in the seat covers like flesh from open wounds. It pained her to see the result of her neglect. She sat in the driver's seat, pulled down the mirror, and, for the first time in years, she looked closely at her face, running her fingertips across the furrows in her forehead, smoothing them out, pushing up with flat palms the skin of her cheeks to iron away the creases that channelled alongside her nose and down to her mouth. Amused at the sudden and positive transformation, she smiled, letting the smile do the face-lift this time. She exhaled, patted the steering wheel, and got out.

When the middle child had returned home some years later, bright T-shirts hid the oozing foam of the seats; new tyres and a new battery had made the wagon hum on the road again, and the middle child was happy to claim it. He and his partner had the body painted orange and designed new chocolate, blue, orange and yellow striped seat covers, piled surfboards on the roof rack, and the wagon was rejuvenated. When that adventurous pair took it from Chaguaramas to Guayaguayare and Matelot to Cedros, the wagon turned heads. People everywhere stared, waved and called out, "All you selling that car? No? Well, when you selling it, call me." The ashtrays filled up with scraps of paper bearing phone numbers. But, when their child was born, the wagon didn't fit their life any more. "The seatbelts at the back can't take a baby's car seat... we tried all the car accessories places... nobody can change these belts for the right ones." And so the wagon came back home to rest, an object of curiosity to passers-by. Eventually, the battery died, the rust erupted through the new paint, and a slick of mould dulled the interior. Still the enquiries continued; the pantomime of calling out, showing, taking numbers and refusing offers went on for almost two years.

Then, in the week of the anniversary of her widowhood, she had been feeling her husband's presence very intensely; she had been consciously trying to tap into the sense of order and practicality that her daily life had lacked in his absence. She remembered that before he had even an inkling of the disease that was to take him, he'd been trying to get her to agree to sell the wagon.

"It's more than twelve years old now," he'd insisted; "let's get you a new car – another wagon."

"But it's not giving any trouble," she'd countered. "Why get rid of it?"

"You going to wait till it starts to give trouble?"

On the anniversary day of his death, the midday post brought a sheaf of white envelopes. The logos announced a phone bill, a water bill, an electricity bill and a cable bill. She recognised the insurance broker's renewal notices for the two cars. Two cars, she said to herself, two cars to insure and fix up and take for testing... one on the road, one parked up... that can't make sense. She surveyed them both as she opened the post, reading it right there in the carport, placing the envelopes and their scanned contents on the trunk lid of the "on the road" car. The parked-up wagon, its wing mirrors besmirched with bird droppings from the kiskedees that perched there for their morning preening, its rear window coated with a deep layer of Sahara dust, looked neglected, unloved. It hurt her to see it like this, to know that this time she could have done better by it. She picked up the post, walked through the kitchen, continued along the cool dark corridor to the bedroom of her marriage, and dropped the post on the low trunk at the foot of her bed where her husband's photo smiled at her. She stood and, looking at the photo, said silently to him, it's starting to give me trouble, so should I...? She searched his face. Did his smile broaden? Did he wink? She thought so. She leaned over and touched his face, saying in herself but to him, yes... you're right, it's time. She pulled open the drawer that still housed his handkerchiefs and socks, chose a pair of his tennis socks and retraced her steps to the front yard.

There, with one old tennis sock as a glove in one hand, hosepipe in the other, she rubbed over the wagon's body – the scarred roof with its run-off grooves and loose chrome strip, the lacklustre doors, the heavy trunk door, the chrome metal back bumper missing one end-rubber, the windscreen, its rubber seal gone rigid, the still bright bonnet, the chrome radiator grille, the two round faithful headlamps – never changed a bulb in a quarter century, the heavy chrome metal front bumper dimpled at one end – they don't make them so again, the number plates with their faded numbers and letters, the hardly-worn tyres. At the end she stood, away from the wagon, her wrap clinging and dripping around her body, her face and hair streaming.

She had hardly had a shower and changed when the bell at the gate rang and there was this little, plump man with the plump, soft hands holding a cap. He wore a benign, gentle smile as if not altogether in the here-and-now. She saw that the rim of his cap had pressed a deep ring-shaped dent into the back of his Friar-Tuck Afro hairstyle, as if his halo fitted too tight. She smiled to herself.

"Yes, it's for sale. You want to come and look at it?" He nodded, came in and simply strolled around the wagon, smiling all the while.

"You want to look inside? It can't start because the battery run down."

"No, I see what I want to see already."

"This car never give me a day's trouble in twenty-five years."

"I know. I hear about this car from your mechanic. I does sew clothes for his madam. I bringing my own mechanic tomorrow."

Next morning he was at the gate with his mechanic and a battery. They changed the battery, changed the plugs, put in some gas, ran the engine for a few minutes and drove the wagon away with a promise to meet at the Licensing Office the following day to make the official change of ownership.

When she saw the wagon in the inspection queue next day it was already somebody else's. There was this stranger in the driver's seat – an absent-minded looking man in his mid-sixties, wearing a cap. He motioned her to get in beside him, but she turned away to hide the revulsion she felt, not at him, but at herself. She felt as if she was agreeing to the putting down of a beloved, loyal pet who had become inconvenient and she couldn't bring herself to face the betrayal by looking in its eyes or stroking its head one last time. When they left Licensing he said, "I bringing it for you to see when I fix it up. I see you don't want it to go." She nodded, too choked-up to speak, and went off to the bank with her thirty pieces of silver.

ABOUT THE AUTHOR

Barbara Magdalena Lafond was born in Belmont on 4th December 1941, the first of Yvonne Lafond's four children. In 1953, she won an exhibition to St Joseph's Convent, POS, then Trinidad's most prestigious Catholic secondary school for girls. On graduating, she accepted a teaching position at the school for a further two years, leaving the country in 1962 on a government scholarship to read Geography at the University College of Wales, Aberystwyth.

In April 1965, in her final year, she married Paul David Jenkins, a fellow graduate. They settled in Cardiff where Barbara obtained her Diploma in Education and worked as a supply teacher. In 1969 their first child, Rhiannon was born. In 1971 they had to relocate to Trinidad to fulfil the terms of her scholarship that required her to teach in the government secondary school system for five years. This period extended until her retirement some twenty-six years later. Meantime, the Jenkins family grew with the birth of Gareth (1973) and Carys (1978). In 1995, while the two older children were in the UK and the youngest still at school in Trinidad, Paul died of cancer in London.

In addition to teaching, Barbara was involved in the preparation of textbooks for schools in the CARICOM region to combat the negative impact of HIV and AIDS; and in giving a Caribbean voice to textbooks written originally for African audiences.

Since 1998, she has belonged to a book club, and served on the executive of the local Dyslexia Association. She is a chorister with the Lydian Singers and Steel, one of the country's foremost choirs, led by the legendary Pat Bishop until 2011, and committed to outreach and community building.

From the year she read all the books in the small, one-room public library in Belmont, books have always been at the heart of her life. Alice Munro, Graham Greene, Derek Walcott, Margaret Atwood, Jean Rhys, Gabriel Garcia Marquez, John Le Carre sustained husband and wife. The dusty relics of these forays, crammed into bookshelves everywhere, are now so much a part of her life, she thinks it would be impossible to part with them.

Her writing life was always an unobserved backdrop. Letters to pen-pals selected from the back pages of American comic books, letters back home in the first UK decade, letters to her in-law family in her Trinidad years and to her children while they were students in the UK were a normal part of life in the era of expensive land-lines before Skype.

Real writing came much later. It was around 2007 when two female friends invited Barbara to join them in a creative writing exercise. They met once a month, to read and to critique whatever they had produced. Out of that experience came the embryos of some of the stories in this collection. She asked a young friend and neighbour, Nicholas Laughlin, editor of the *Caribbean Review of Books*, to read one of her stories. He reported that he really liked it and encouraged her to apply, successfully, for a place at the Cropper Foundation Residential Creative Writing Workshop in 2008. In the Commonwealth Short Story Competition in 2009 her entry was highly commended. She won their Caribbean Region Prize in 2010 and 2011, was shortlisted in the first *Wasafiri* New Writing Prize, 2009, and winner of their Life Writing Prize, 2010. This was followed by The Canute Brodhurst Prize for short fiction 2010, from *The Caribbean Writer*, winner of the short story competition, *Small Axe*, 2011, winner of the Romance Category, My African Diaspora Short Story Contest, 2010, and the inaugural The Caribbean Communications Network (CCN) Prize for a film review of the Trinidad and Tobago Film Festival, 2012.

In 2010 she enrolled at the University of The West Indies, St Augustine Campus, to read for the MFA in Creative Writing under Professor Funso Aiyejina. She graduated with high commendation in 2012.

Barbara now lives in Diego Martin, an outer suburb of Port of Spain. While it can take upwards of an hour to commute to the city through almost stagnant traffic, exhaust fumes, gridlocked intersections and a dull urbanscape, going in the opposite direction for about the same distance takes her through fishing villages, brisk salty breezes, rainforest-clad mountain and sea views to the greeny-gold waters of Macqueripe Bay in just twelve minutes. She leaves early morning critical decision making to her car. Hot afternoons find her in a shady verandah, stretched out in a Colombian hammock, with a tumbler of coconut water fortified with rum in one hand and a good book made out of paper and imagination in the other.

OTHER RECENT TRINIDADIAN FICTION

Raymond Ramcharitar
The Island Quintet: Five Stories
ISBN: 9781845230753; pp. 232; pub. 2009; £8.99

Raymond Ramcharitar's vision is rooted in Trinidad, but as a globalised island with permeable borders, frequent birds of passage, and outposts in New York and London. One of the collection's outstanding qualities is that it is both utterly contemporary and written with a profound and disturbed sense of the history that shapes the island. As befits fiction from the home of carnival and mas', it is a collection much concerned with the flesh – often in transgressive forms as if characters are driven to test their boundaries – and with the capacity of its characters to reinvent themselves in manifold, and sometimes outrageous disguises. One of the masks is race, and the stories are acerbically honest about the way tribal loyalties distort human relations. Its tone ranges from the lyric – Trinidad as an island of arresting beauty – to a seaminess of the most grungy kind. It has an ambition that challenges a novel such as V.S. Naipaul's *The Mimic Men*, but is written with the anger and the compassion of a writer for whom the island still means everything. In the novella, "Froude's Arrow", Ramcharitar has written a profound fiction that tells us where the Caribbean currently is in juxtaposing the deep, still to be answered questions about island existence (the fragmentations wrought by history, the challenges of smallness in the global market, race and class divides) and the scrabbling for survival, fame and fortune that arouse the ire of Ramcharitar's acerbic and satirical vision.

Keith Jardim
Near Open Water
ISBN: 9781845231880; pp. 168; pub. 2011; £8.99

These stories present, in writing that is both meticulous and poetic, a Caribbean world of unparalleled natural beauty, and societies that seethe on the edge of chaos, where crime encompasses both the rulers and the ruled, and where representatives of the state are as out of control as the youth Cynthia witnesses hacking off the hand of an old woman in a casual robbery. We enter this world through the perceptions of both those struggling for survival at the base of society and members of the old elite facing the consequences of past privilege in the reality of present insecurity. The stories stare hard into the abyss, at times taking us to hallucinatory places where nothing is certain. What is certain is the energy and precision in the stories' subtle edge of moral rigour in exploring the inner lives of those who fail to see that their "minor" deceits and evasions contribute to the "fire in the city". In such sympathetically drawn characters as Nello, the former car-thief now trying to do the right thing, or the memorably eccentric Dr Edric Traboulay with his intimate relationship to the natural world, we are offered glimpses of possibility. This is fiction that calls a society to see itself clearly, though about the revelatory power of writing the author is modestly ambivalent, as the powerful title story so shockingly reveals.

'The sense of place is fabulous, interweaving vistas of landscape and seascape, local fauna and flora, architecture, politics, inhabitants, history... all of which creates an atmosphere of longing and despair – despair at the impossibility of ever achieving what is longed for... The stories play nicely with the disjunction between place as redemptive and place as punitive/purgatorial. The sense of foreboding that pervades all of the stories is impelled by this tension... the work is "postcolonial" in the very best sense of that critical label.'

Lois Parkinson Zamora